THE DRAGON REALM

DARK WORLD: THE DRAGON TWINS 2

MICHELLE MADOW

DREAMSCAPE PUBLISHING

1

GEMMA

I STEPPED inside the Eternal Library, spun around, and stared at the door.

Come on, Ethan. I could barely breathe as I waited for him to come through. Time felt like it stood still.

There were five more demons in that room that we hadn't killed.

Had they gotten to him? Stopped him from leaving? Or worse?

Had he decided to stay back and kill them all himself? He'd been so angry. And after what he'd learned about Lavinia killing his dad, I nearly slapped myself for not considering the possibility that he might stay back for revenge.

You'll be right behind me? I remembered the words I'd spoken to him only seconds earlier.

Always.

I hadn't questioned his response.

Because I trusted Ethan with all of my soul. The Ethan in this reality… the Ethan in my dreams… he was the same. I'd felt it when I'd kissed him.

Finally, when I was seconds away from putting my key back in the lock and returning to that room, Ethan hurried out of the door.

I rushed into his arms and buried my face in his chest, inhaling his familiar, earthy scent. His arms tightened around me, warm after using his fire magic.

"What took you so long?" I asked after pulling away.

"It's only been a few seconds."

"Oh." It felt like it had been so much longer.

I stood there, speechless, my eyes locked on his hazel ones. Then, my focus drifted down to his lips.

The lips I'd kissed.

His breathing shallowed, as if he was thinking about the kiss, too.

"That wasn't the first time," he said slowly.

"What do you mean?"

"We've kissed before. I don't know how to explain it, but I *remember* it. Kind of. It's hazy, like a dream…" He shook his head and looked off to the side, then snapped his focus back to me. "I probably sound crazy."

"No," I said quickly. "You don't."

"Did you feel it, too?"

I swallowed, since where could I possibly begin? How was I supposed to explain my experience to him, when I didn't understand it myself?

"What do you remember?" I asked instead.

"The two of us, kissing in the cove," he said, his cheeks flushed. "In the library at school. In the back room in the café. In your room." His eyes roamed up and down my body, and heat rose to my cheeks, too.

Because what we'd done together in my room had been far more than kissing.

"It doesn't make sense." He scratched his head. "Unless..."

"Unless what?"

"Memory potion." He dropped his arm back down to his side and stood straighter. "Witches can make memory potion and use it to take away memories and replace them with false ones. Like what they did to Raven."

I nodded, since I knew all about what had happened to Raven—both from the textbook on the history of the supernatural world, and from the Queen of Swords herself.

She'd been taken by a witch and held captive in a prison for weeks. Afterward, she'd been given memory potion to make her forget the supernatural world. Her memories had been replaced, so she'd believed she'd jetted off to Europe and spent all of that time there, instead of being locked in a witch's prison.

Which would mean…

"You think your time with Mira wasn't real?" As I said it, I *wished* it were true.

I was a terrible sister.

"I don't know." He shrugged. "They feel real. More real than what I remember with you."

His words sent a sharp pain through my chest.

"What else do you remember with me?" I held my breath again, wishing for the impossible.

Wishing for him to remember *all* of it.

"No more than I just told you," he said. "And the memories are already fading. But maybe Hecate knows what's going on." He looked around the Library's ivory hall, but I'd already checked—Hecate wasn't there.

I'd been to the Eternal Library enough times by now to realize that Hecate usually wasn't there. It was like she was teasing us. Because the library contained endless knowledge, but only when she saw it fit to provide it to us.

"I'm sorry." Guilt filled me deep to the core as I thought about how I'd rushed up to him and kissed him. "I shouldn't have done it. I just didn't know what else to do…" I flashed back to Ethan standing there, staring at

Jamie's corpse—at where he'd driven the dagger into her heart. He'd been lost in his mind, oblivious to the demons prowling the boundary dome around us. "I needed to bring you back."

He looked across the hall, and his grip tightened around the handle of the sword sheathed by his side. "She's going to pay for what she did," he said, his voice dark and deadly. "I'm going to carve out Lavinia's heart and make sure she's awake to feel every excruciating moment of it."

I wished so badly that I could take his pain away. Instead, I swallowed, unsure what to say.

"I'm the ruler of my people now—no matter how few are left of us." He still wasn't looking at me. It was like he was talking to himself, figuring out his thoughts aloud. So, despite my multitude of questions, I did what I thought he needed, and waited silently for him to continue. "I need to go to them. I need to free them. And then, we'll attack the demons. Rip them apart until there's not a single one of them left. They're going to beg for mercy, and they'll curse the day that they thought they could get away with bringing the dragons into this war."

He spun back around, and I flinched at the vengeful glint in his eyes.

Then he shook it off and was back to the warm,

caring Ethan I knew and loved. "But first, we need to get back to the Ward."

I nodded and reached for my key.

The longer we stayed here, the more I feared that Ethan might want answers so badly that I'd lose him to the Library's endless halls.

"And Gemma?" he said, and I froze, waiting for him to continue. "Promise me something."

"Anything."

"Don't tell Mira. If she finds out, it'll break her."

"I know," I said, since while my twin was strong, she had one major weakness.

Ethan.

And I was going to make sure she never found out that he was my biggest weakness, too.

2

GEMMA

I STEPPED through the library door first, and emerged in the guest common room of the Ward.

As we'd discussed, Mira and Makena were waiting for us there. Mira paced around, running her fingers down a strand of her short blond hair. Makena sat at the head of the table, perfectly still.

Mira stopped walking, and her wide blue eyes met mine.

Guilt washed over me again. My chest hurt—it was like someone had taken a belt, wrapped it around my ribcage, and kept tightening it until I was going to explode.

I'd never be able to look at my twin the same way again. And if she knew about me and Ethan...

She'd hate me.

I wished I didn't think it possible that my twin could ever hate me. But she'd become so obsessed with Ethan that it was like she loved him more than me.

I didn't have much time to continue spiraling in my downward thoughts, because Ethan entered the room a few seconds after me.

Mira's eyes lit up, and she ran into his arms.

He hugged her back, but his eyes were blank, as if he felt nothing.

Finally, after a few painful seconds of watching the two of them together, Mira pulled away and looked up at Ethan. "Harper?" she asked, and she glanced to me, waiting for one of us to answer.

I shook my head no, unable to say it out loud.

Harper's dead.

I couldn't save her.

We left her behind.

But Harper had already stopped breathing when we'd left her. And she'd chosen to fight those demons, even though we had a clear path to the door.

Still, I should have reacted faster to help her. If I had, maybe she'd be here.

"Let's sit down." Ethan led Mira to the table, and they sat side by side.

I sat across from Ethan and stared down at my hands, unable to look at him. If I did, I was sure my sister would see my love for him splattered across my face.

Makena cleared her throat. "Explain what happened," she said.

Ethan took the lead, telling them everything that had happened from the moment we'd been dropped off in Lilith's lair.

"I'm sorry to hear about your father," Makena said once he was finished. "From what I've heard, he was an excellent king."

Ethan nodded. "His footsteps will be impossible to fill."

"It will be difficult," Makena said. "But every leader brings his or her people in a new direction. I have confidence that you'll make your father proud."

"I'll have to, eventually," he said. "But the Elders lead our people—*my* people—whenever my father's gone. And he was gone more than he was there, so he could be here on Earth looking after me and my sister. We were always his priority." He looked to Mira, and then to me. "Because my job is to look after the two of you. And the two of you are my people's priority."

"They believe we're destined to save them," I said, remembering what he'd told us after we'd received our magic. Then I remembered what Isobel—the dark witch being held captive in the Ward—had told us before we'd left. "The dragons in Ember are slaves. And they think we can free them."

"Which is why the two of you are a priority," Ethan said. "By keeping you alive, I'm ensuring the freedom of my people."

My first instinct was to say that Mira and I weren't strong enough to save a realm of enslaved dragons. But I pressed my lips together, keeping the thought to myself.

Because right now, Ethan needed something to believe in. He needed a purpose.

That purpose was me and Mira.

I stole a glance at him, surprised to find he was looking straight at me.

I looked away as quickly as possible.

Luckily, Mira was focused on the door we'd both came in through.

"Why did Harper do it?" she asked. "The two of you were holding off the demons with your magic. You gave her a straight path out of there. She knew you could hold them back long enough to follow after her. So why'd she fight them?"

"Harper was angry." Makena's voice was hard and firm. "Lilith's dark army destroyed her home and killed nearly everyone she knew. Harper was also an extremely strong witch—not just for someone her age, but for *any* witch. It made her arrogant. Anger and arrogance don't mesh together well."

"Don't talk about her that way," I snapped.

Makena barely reacted. "I'm simply answering your sister's question."

I glared at her in response.

Everyone in the Ward was so cold and unfeeling. I couldn't wait to get out of there.

"Harper was right to be angry," Ethan said, and from the steady way he spoke, I could tell it was taking him every effort to contain his anger, too. "But Makena's right. Harper was impulsive, and it got her killed. I won't let either of you make that same mistake."

"We won't," Mira said quickly. "Especially because we have no reason to go back there."

"I don't just mean there," Ethan said. "I mean *anywhere*. Lilith might not be able to track you through your magic anymore, but she's still after you. You won't be safe until she's dead."

"But only a Nephilim can kill a greater demon," Mira said. "We literally *can't* kill her. And neither can you."

"We might not be able to make the killing blow," Ethan said. "But there are other ways we can help."

"Such as what?"

"Firstly, by freeing the dragons in Ember," he said.

"But more immediately, by going to the Eternal Library and asking Hecate."

Makena looked unsurprised by Ethan's statement.

It was like she hadn't heard him at all.

"Now that no one can track you when you use your dragon magic, your time is best spent practicing in the Haven," she said. "The three of you are too powerful to spend your time with your noses stuck in books. There are plenty of other supernaturals who have that task covered."

So, she didn't have a key.

The keys were spelled so that whenever someone with a key mentioned the secrets of the Library to someone without a key, the person without a key forgot immediately—or, in Makena's case, thought they'd heard something else.

She seemed to think that Ethan wanted us to search for information in various supernatural libraries, instead of getting information from Hecate in her Eternal Library.

"Don't worry," Ethan said. "We'll be practicing."

She nodded in approval.

"Thank you for letting us stay here these past few days," I added, in an attempt to change the subject.

"It was the least I could do to thank you for bringing us a witch from Lilith's army," Makena said.

I looked down at my hands.

Because *Harper* had been the one to bring Isobel to the Ward. Makena should have been thanking Harper —not us.

Ethan stood up. "It's best we be on our way," he said, and then he turned to me and Mira. "There's someone in the Haven who's going to be *very* happy to see you."

"Mom." I smiled, although it vanished a second later.

Because Mom would ask why Harper wasn't with us.

Telling her about what had happened would be like re-living it all over again.

"Is there anything I can get you before you teleport out?" Makena asked.

"No," I said, not bothering to say that we weren't strong enough witches to teleport—that we'd be using our keys. She'd simply forget a second later and return to her belief that we'd be teleporting away. "We're good."

And then, one by one, the three of us used our keys to step through the common room door and into the Eternal Library.

3

GEMMA

HECATE WASN'T THERE.

Since it hadn't been long since we'd been in the Library, I shouldn't have expected anything else. But the keys couldn't be used to travel directly from one place to another—we always needed to stop in the Library as an in-between. So it didn't hurt to hope.

After doing a final look around to make sure Hecate wasn't hiding behind any bookshelves, we returned to the tearoom in the Haven.

The guard stationed outside the door sent a fire message to Mary to alert her of our arrival.

Minutes later, Mary entered the room, with Mom and Raven at her heels.

"Where's Harper?" Raven was the first to ask the question.

"She's gone," I said blankly, and then we sat down and told them everything that had happened in that room with the demons.

Mom was crying by the time we were done. Only a few tears—she quickly wiped them off her cheeks—but I didn't think I'd ever seen her cry. Parents were supposed to be the strong ones, and Mom had always been stronger than most.

She'd also always been the one to take care of me and Mira. But now that Mira and I had magic, and Mom still barely had any, we were the ones who needed to protect her.

The role reversal couldn't be easy on her.

"What's your plan from here?" Raven asked once they were caught up on what had happened.

"We're going to do everything we can to kill Lilith," Ethan said.

"So you want to go to Avalon."

"I thought Avalon only accepted the strongest supernaturals," Mom said.

"Avalon accepts anyone who passes the island's Trials," Raven said. "Usually that means the strongest supernaturals and humans—so the humans can train to become Nephilim. But not always. There's not an exact science behind it. But it doesn't hurt to try."

I glanced at the others, unsure what to say. Because

since getting attacked in the cove, all we'd been focused on was learning how to use our magic and figuring out how Lilith was tracking us. We hadn't thought about where we'd go afterward.

Where *were* we supposed to go?

We wouldn't fit in at the café in Australia anymore. Going back there and pretending everything was normal would be impossible.

I'd started to think of Utopia as home—or at least as a place that could eventually be my home—but that had been yanked away when Utopia was destroyed.

Perhaps Avalon was a good choice.

But what if all four of us didn't pass Avalon's Trials? Then I wouldn't be able to stay. Because I wouldn't feel at home without Mom and Mira... and without Ethan.

Of course, that was assuming I'd pass the Trials. Maybe I'd fail.

"It's something to think about," Ethan finally said. "But first, we have some questions we need answered."

"No better place to get questions answered than at Avalon," Raven said. "We don't have anyone on the island with dragon magic. I'm sure Annika will be happy to sit down with you and chat."

Annika—the only full angel that lived on Earth. They called her the Earth Angel. She was also the Queen of Cups, which meant she could use the Holy Grail to turn humans into Nephilim. *And* she was the leader of Avalon.

She was probably even more intimidating than Raven.

"I thought Annika didn't know anything about the Dark Objects?" I asked.

"She doesn't," Mary said. "According to Annika, the Dark Objects aren't supposed to exist. She was more surprised to hear about them than I was."

Raven turned back to me and Mira. "By coming to Avalon, you'll be part of Avalon's Army," she continued, and then she focused on Ethan. "What better way to help us kill Lilith than that?"

"Dragons are strong fighters. I can help kill Lilith by freeing my people," he said. "And we can't do that from Avalon."

"You can't do that from here, either."

"I never said we intended to get our questions answers here."

"Then how do you plan to get them answered?"

"By using this." Ethan pulled his key out from under his shirt. "I'm going into Hecate's Eternal Library every morning until she shows up and tells me what I need to know."

Raven blinked, her eyes blank.

Mira fiddled with the chain around her neck.

"Raven," Mary said gently, and Raven looked to her, as if she hadn't heard a word Ethan had said. "The four of them have been on the run to stay alive for weeks. Give them time. This isn't a decision that needs to be made this exact second."

"I don't know about that," Raven said. "Even though Lilith doesn't have a vampire who tracks dragon magic anymore, she's not going to stop coming after the twins. And Avalon is the safest place in the world. Not even the Dark Wand can break through Avalon's barriers."

"How do you know that?" I asked.

"Because if it could, Lavinia would have used it already. Just like she did on Utopia."

"Unless Lilith has a bigger plan."

"A bigger plan than taking down Avalon?" Raven scoffed. "I highly doubt that."

"Raven," Mary said sternly. "We're tabling this discussion for now. They've been through a lot these past few days. Give them time to process."

I relaxed slightly, since Mary was right. The past few days felt like they'd happened in a blur. We needed time to think.

And time to talk to Hecate.

"Fine," Raven gave in. "Take time to think. But during that time, we're going to continue our training."

Mira groaned, and I couldn't blame her. Raven's sword fighting lessons were *exhausting*.

"Not as intensely as before, since I'm assuming you'll also be practicing using your elemental magic," she continued. "But you still need to train to fight. Because even though you can use your magic now without being tracked, it doesn't change the fact that the only way to kill a demon is with a holy weapon. Which means you have to get as good at using them as possible."

4

GEMMA

My thoughts were so consumed with my memories of Ethan that I couldn't fall asleep that night.

No, not memories.

Of my *dream* of Ethan.

Or my drug-induced hallucination of Ethan.

Whatever it was.

But even though he'd remembered, his memories had slipped away.

Maybe, if we kissed again, they'd return.

But what if they disappeared every time? I'd have my Ethan back for a few minutes, and then he'd disappear, over and over and over again.

It would be torture. Self-inflicted torture.

Maybe it would be worth it for those few minutes of happiness.

Maybe his memories would come back stronger each time, until they were ingrained in his soul as permanently as they were ingrained in mine?

But I'd never find out. Because what had happened in that room could never happen again. We'd both agreed on it.

I couldn't do that to Mira.

It would be so much easier if I could forget about the Ethan I'd loved, as easily as he'd forgotten about me.

Then, I gasped. Because maybe I could.

I instantly gave up on trying to sleep, got up, and got dressed. Because there was someone I needed to see.

And I needed to see her *now*.

The doors in the Haven didn't have locks, but when I held my key up to the doorknob, a lock magically appeared above it. I clicked it open, and stepped into the Eternal Library.

As always, I looked for Hecate.

She wasn't there.

So I opened the Library door again and walked through, ending up on the front step of the person's house I was going to see.

I felt bad for waking her up at noon, which was the

equivalent to the middle of the night in the Haven, since all vampire kingdoms kept a nocturnal schedule. But this conversation couldn't wait.

So I knocked on the door.

Rosella answered in a second. She wore Haven whites, and her dark hair was secured in a loose braid that flowed down her back. Her milky eyes were pointed in my direction, although they were blank and unfocused.

"Come in." She opened the door wider and motioned for me to enter. "I've been expecting you."

Of course she'd been expecting me. I supposed that was one of the perks of having future sight.

I inhaled the sweet, sugary scent of pancakes and syrup, and smiled. The kitchen table was already set for two people, with a plate stacked high with pancakes in the center. I rarely ate pancakes—Mom said pancakes, waffles, and French toast were excuses to eat dessert for breakfast—so I welcomed the treat.

A cup full of blood sat next to Rosella's water glass, and a mug of white hot chocolate was next to mine.

"Given what you're going through, I figured you needed some comfort food," she explained as she sat down.

I also took my seat. "Do I even need to explain why I'm here?"

"Please do. I have a general idea about what's going on, but only from an outsider's perspective. For a better understanding, it would help to hear it from you. And since you haven't spoken with anyone about it yet, I feel like it would help you to talk about it, too."

And so, I launched into everything that had happened since being poisoned by the nightshade, talking so quickly that I barely had time to drink my hot chocolate, let alone eat pancakes. But the whole situation was making me so anxious that I didn't have much of an appetite, anyway.

"Have you ever remembered a dream so clearly before?" Rosella asked when I was done.

"No. I have intense dreams a lot, but they always fade, like dreams are supposed to."

"Then your experience doesn't sound like a dream."

"I know that," I said. "But if it wasn't a dream, then what was it?"

"What do *you* think it was?"

"I don't know." I let out a long, frustrated breath and stabbed my pancake with my fork. "That's why I'm asking you."

"Your intuition is strong. I'd like to hear what you think."

"My thought sounds crazy." I'd barely even let *myself* think it, since it was too out there to possibly be true.

She cocked her head to the side. "Crazier than everything that's happened in the past few months?"

"Yep," I said. "Definitely crazier."

"Then I'm all ears."

"All right." I said, sitting forward. "Have you ever heard about the multiverse theory?"

"The theory that there are an infinite number of worlds running parallel to ours, each the result of a different decision we've made."

"I guess that means you've heard of it."

"I can see the future." She smiled. "But I only see the future as it would turn out at that point in time. The moment I share a person's future with them, they can make a different decision and change the future I previously saw. So I know more than anyone that there are *many* ways life can play out."

"But is there only one way it can play out? Or does each decision cause a split, so it plays out in both ways, but in different worlds?"

"You think there's another world where you opened up to Ethan in the cove, and he ended up with you instead of your sister? And that the nightshade allowed you to experience that world?"

It sounded crazy when she said it out loud.

"Is it possible?" I asked.

"I wish I had an answer, but I'm afraid I don't know,"

she said sadly. "However, what I do know is this—you exist in *this* world, and the past is set in stone. You create your own future here. What point is there in wondering what your life would be like if you made a different decision in the past?"

"I don't know." I shrugged. "But maybe if nightshade brought me there once, it can bring me there again."

"If there are an infinite number of worlds, how can you guarantee that taking the nightshade would take you to the exact same world you experienced before?" she asked, although she continued before I could answer. "Even if you could return to that world, you had no control of your body in there. Would you want to be a parasite living inside this other version of yourself forever? And if you did choose that, what would happen to your actual body here?"

"You're making my head spin."

"I'd say I can't imagine it, but I see a future that's regularly changing, so I'm not one to talk," she said. "But tell me—how have these memories been making you feel?"

"Sad," I said without a second thought. "Alone. Confused. I'm grieving a relationship that no one else knows about. One that technically never existed—at least not in this world. And I can't talk about it with anyone. Except now, with you."

"And I'm more than happy to listen," she said. "But you came here to ask me a question."

"I just asked you a ton of questions."

"But you haven't asked *the* question. The one I can actually answer."

I took a deep breath. Because once I asked, there was no turning back from the decision I'd have to make.

"If I took memory potion, would it erase my memories of what I experienced with Ethan?"

I held my breath, unsure what I wanted the answer to be.

If she said no, then I wouldn't have to decide if I wanted to take the potion or not. It would be decided for me.

If she said yes... then I'd forget how incredible it felt to be loved by Ethan. How safe and cared for I was with him.

That would be a good thing, I reminded myself. *It's what I want.*

Was it?

"Yes," Rosella answered, giving me no sign if she thought this was a good idea or not. "It would."

"Do you have some for me?" I wouldn't be surprised if she did, since she knew why I wanted to talk to her before I'd arrived.

"I don't," she said. "Only an extremely powerful

witch can brew a strong enough memory potion to do what you ask. And one of the ingredients she'll need will be a bit of your DNA, such as a strand of hair."

"I don't know the high witches here," I said. "At least, not well enough to make this request."

The only one I'd known well had been Harper. I swallowed down a lump in my throat at the thought of her.

I also knew Makena, but I had a sense she wasn't the type of person to do anything for free.

"Do you think you can introduce me to one here in the Haven?" I asked. "One you know I can trust?"

"I don't need to introduce you to a Haven high witch," Rosella said simply. "Because there's one you already know."

I wracked my mind trying to think of a high witch I'd had an actual conversation with in my time in the Haven. But for the majority of the time I'd been here, I'd either been training with Raven, or sleeping. I'd met some witches in passing, but that was all.

"She's not currently living in the Haven," Rosella continued. "And you met her before going to Utopia."

Where was I before going to Utopia?

Home.

"Shivani," I said the name of the Haven high witch who was watching the café while we were gone.

"Yes." Rosella nodded. "You'll get to her. I don't know how—since your magic isn't strong enough for you to teleport—but I know you will."

I reached for the chain around my neck. "I take it that means you don't know about Hecate's keys."

I assumed not—since she wasn't a witch—but it didn't hurt to try. Maybe her future sight gave her insight that no one else had.

Rosella was quiet for a second. Then she shook her head, as if coming out of a daze. "I'm sorry," she said. "What did you just say?"

"Hecate's keys," I tried again.

She said nothing. It was like she hadn't heard me at all.

"You're right," I said, giving up. "I can figure out a way to get there on my own."

"I know you will. But memory potion takes a bit of time to brew, so you should get going. You don't want anyone to realize you're gone. If they do, they might start asking questions."

She was right. I'd never been a good liar, especially when it came to lying to Mira.

Which was why I *needed* to take the memory potion.

If I didn't remember being in love with Ethan, then I wouldn't have to lie about it. And I'd feel better, too. I wouldn't have this aching hole in my heart that no one would ever be able to fill.

But that nagging feeling still tugged at my soul. The one asking if I truly wanted to forget the greatest love I'd ever known.

"I'm going to decide to take the potion, right?" I asked Rosella.

If I knew what I'd do, then I could stop wondering and worrying.

"The decision is yours, and yours alone," she said. "If I tell you the future I see now, it could influence you to make a completely different decision. All you can do is what you feel is right. Not just for you, but for everyone involved."

I cursed inwardly. Of course it couldn't be as easy as her telling me the right choice to make.

"You best get a move on," she said, and she stood up to see me out. "The clock is ticking, and time waits for no one."

5

GEMMA

ROSELLA SAID GOODBYE, and she closed the door, leaving me on her doorstep.

I reached for my key necklace and stared at the lock.

I needed to get this over with. I'd feel so much better after I did.

So I stuck the key into the lock, turned it, and stepped into the ivory hall of the Eternal Library.

Hecate wasn't there. But I didn't mind, since she wasn't who I needed to see. Talking to her would waste time I didn't have.

I turned back around and stared at the door I'd just come in through. Using the key was easy—I just had to picture the place where I wanted to go. And, other than my room at home, there was no easier place for me to picture than the café downstairs. The old wooden floorboards, the shelves of books that lined the walls, and the tables surrounded by chairs and sofas. It was warm and homey—nothing like the chain coffee shops people loved in the city. When people came to Twin Pines Café, it was to sit down, *enjoy* their drink, and appreciate the view of the ocean from the back porch or outside the window.

I could almost smell the fresh coffee.

When I stepped through the door, everything was just as I remembered. It was dinner time, so the evening crowd was enjoying their sandwiches and drinks, along with plenty of tourists who'd stopped by at the end of their scenic drive along John Astor Road.

"Gemma!" someone said from one of the couches near the bookshelves. "You're back!"

My best friend from school, Jillian. She was up in a second, and nearly gave me a hug. Then she froze, her eyes running up and down my clothes.

"What are you wearing?" she asked.

I looked down at my Haven whites, feeling stupid for not remembering to change.

"Long story," I said, and I hurried toward the door to the back room. As far as I knew, Shivani had told everyone that my family and I had moved in with relatives in New Zealand. I did *not* have time to coordinate with her cover story right now. "I'm only here for a bit. Sorry."

I disappeared into the back room, not giving her time to ask any more questions.

Hopefully Shivani could make a memory potion for Jillian, so she'd forget I was there. Slip it in her coffee or something. The taste of the coffee was strong enough that it might be able to mask the potion, especially on someone who wasn't expecting it.

I hurried upstairs to Mom's room/office. Shivani was there on the computer, managing the bookkeeping, just like Mom would have been doing if we'd been home.

She looked up from the computer, startled. "Gemma," she said, and she glanced around, checking to see if anyone else was there. "What are you doing here?"

"I need memory potion," I said quickly. "And I don't want anyone to know about it."

"So you came to me."

"Obviously." I was so eager to get this over with that I could barely stand still.

"All right," she said. "But if I'm making you memory potion, then I need to know what for."

"It's a long story," I said, hating that I had to go over it *again*.

It hurt too much to repeat. Talking about it was like opening a fresh wound.

"Then I suggest you tell me quickly." She leaned back and crossed her legs, clearly not going to budge. "Because I'm not making you a memory potion without knowing *why* I'm making you a memory potion."

I paced around the room and summarized the situation as fast as I could.

Once I finished, Shivani's expression was solemn. "I'm sorry for everything you're going through," she said. "And I'm more than happy to help. It's just..."

My heart dropped. "Just what?"

"I've never heard of nightshade doing such a thing."

"Oh." I frowned.

"But memory potion works on all memories." She forced brightness into her tone. "You have memories of these moments with Ethan. So it doesn't seem illogical to think you can drink memory potion and erase the false memories."

"So I'll replace the false memories with... different false memories."

"Ideally, you won't remember them at all," she said. "It'll be like your experiences while asleep were a forgotten dream. Although, the potion will only erase your memories of the time when you were knocked out from the nightshade. If you want to erase your memory of your kiss with Ethan, I'd have to create a separate potion. Although I don't see what good that would do, since *Ethan* would still remember it. But with your false memories erased, your emotions attached to the kiss should disappear, too."

"Good," I said, although the word felt empty. "That's good."

"I need a strand of your hair."

I plucked one out and handed it to her.

"Perfect," she said. "Now, you look like you could use some sleep."

I yawned, not realizing how tired I was until she said it. And the thought of lying down in my own bed sounded *really* nice.

I'd missed being home.

"Go get some rest," she said. "I'll wake you once the potion's ready."

6

GEMMA

I GOT BACK BEFORE SUNSET, so no one realized I'd left.

For the next two days, Ethan, Mira and I visited the Eternal Library to see if Hecate was there to answer our questions.

She wasn't.

So we continued with our training. Raven didn't give up on telling us about Avalon while we were practicing sword fighting with her. And while life on the island did sound wonderful, the thought of living there didn't feel right to me. I couldn't explain why, but it was like something was tugging me in a different direction. I didn't know where that direction was, but I could pretty confidently say it wasn't Avalon.

"He looks so hot when he fights with a sword," Mira

said, ogling Ethan as he sparred with Raven. "Doesn't he?"

My heart slowed, and my blood froze.

Because it was the tone Mira used when she was egging someone on. But she wasn't even looking at me. Her eyes were glued on Ethan.

Ethan—who *did* always look attractive when fighting with a sword. Especially when he was fighting to keep us safe.

But he hadn't looked at me since we'd returned to the Haven. He'd look in my general direction, but he never met my eyes.

It was worse than when he'd acted like I was a stranger.

Because now I was a stranger whose existence he was purposefully ignoring.

Mira didn't seem to require an answer to her question, which was good, because my throat was so constricted that I wasn't sure I'd be able to speak.

Drink the potion. It'll all be better once you do.

The indestructible vial of memory potion was hidden in my undergarments drawer in my room in the Haven. A cliché place to keep it, but it would be safe there. Especially because everyone in the Haven respected each other's privacy.

Every morning and night, I'd taken it out and stared at it.

And every morning and night, I'd placed it back in the drawer.

I'd gone to all that trouble to get the potion. So why couldn't I do something as simple as *drinking* it?

"Nice job," Raven said, pulling me out of my thoughts. The tip of her sword was pressed against Ethan's chest. "If you'd been fighting anyone else, I bet you would have won."

She lowered her sword, and Ethan held out his hand, shaking hers.

"Good match," he said, and she smirked as she dropped her arm back to her side.

No one could beat the Queen of Swords when it came to fighting with blades. Especially when she was using the Holy Sword, Excalibur—the one she was holding now.

She never parted with it. I'd bet she even slept with it.

"Time to break for the day," Raven said. "I don't know about you guys, but I'm *starving*."

"Me, too," I said, and I turned to walk in the direction of the hotel. "I'll see you tomorrow!" I tried to sound as chipper as I could.

"You're having dinner in your room *again*?" she asked.

Mira waited for my answer, too.

Ethan, of course, wouldn't look at me.

"I'm tired," I said what I'd been saying every night. Training was exhausting, and fighting my feelings for Ethan was even more so. "And I want to do some reading before bed."

I also had zero desire to have dinner with Ethan and Mira. Lunch every day had been tough enough, but at least lunch was quick. In the Haven, they lingered and socialized in the dining hall long after finishing dinner.

Having dinner sent to my room so I could stare at the walls and brood over my feelings for Ethan and whether or not to take the memory potion was clearly a *much* better use of my time. Especially because if I'd just drink it, then I'd stop being so miserable. Maybe I'd even be able to relax and make some friends in the Haven, like Mira had been doing.

"You sure about that?" Raven's eyebrows knitted in concern. And while her reflexes were quick, I could have sworn she'd glanced at Ethan.

Does she know?

There was no way she could know. Except... Raven was observant. She had to be, to anticipate her opponent's every move.

And the sooner I drank that potion, the less there'd be for her to observe.

"I'm sure," I said, and then, like every night since getting back to the Haven, I hurried back to my room.

Except tonight, I intended to finally be able to sleep without tossing and turning over my unrequited love for Ethan.

Because with my memories gone, my heart could finally rest, and I could be at peace.

7

GEMMA

THE NEXT MORNING, it finally happened.

I stepped into the ivory hall of the Eternal Library, and Hecate was there.

She wore a sparkling purple gown, and her raven-colored hair flowed freely down her back. She was so ethereal that she took my breath away.

"You're here," I said, shocked.

"Yes." She gave me a close-lipped, knowing smile. "I'm here."

Mira stepped through the door next, followed by Ethan.

My twin stepped back the moment she saw Hecate, as if intimidated by the goddess's presence.

Ethan reached for her waist and steadied her.

I looked away, since for reasons I didn't understand,

my chest always tightened at the sight of the two of them together.

Probably because of that kiss...

But that hadn't meant anything. At least, not to him. I'd just needed to snap him out of it, and he'd kissed me back because for a moment, he'd thought I was Mira.

It was an accident. I needed to forget about it.

He already had.

So I pushed the thought away and refocused on Hecate.

The goddess was as calm as ever. "I believe you have questions for me?" she asked.

"So many questions," I said quickly.

"Then I hope you've prepared your best ones."

I swallowed, then nodded. Because *Ethan* had his best question ready. From there, my best question depended on Hecate's answer to his question, and then Mira's on her answer to mine.

But I was ready to think on my feet.

"Come with me." Hecate spun around and led us through the door that opened to a never-ending hall lined with bookshelves from top to bottom. A buffet table ran down the center, displaying a variety of food and drinks for those who'd been too impatient to wait for Hecate and had gotten lost wandering the Library, trying to search for the answers to their questions on their own.

How long had they returned to the Library, day after day, before giving up on getting an audience with Hecate and venturing to find a book with the answer to their question themselves?

What question was worth risking the loss of what could be years of their lives?

And why did Hecate appear in the Library some days, and not on other days? And why would she only answer our questions if she met us in the ivory hall, and not if we were lost perusing the endless books on the shelves?

But I wasn't going to ask any of those questions. At least, not today. Because the answers wouldn't help the situation on Earth. And saving Earth was the number one priority.

"Who wants to go first?" Hecate asked.

She'd barely finished speaking before Ethan stepped forward.

"How do we kill Lilith?" he asked, his voice low and deadly. His eyes gleamed with spite—with his need for revenge.

I was grateful he was on my side, and not fighting against me. Because anyone in Ethan's path was bound to get burned by the dragon king.

It was so surreal that he was an actual *king*.

Hecate gazed down the hall. Her eyes swirled purple like the night sky, and mist poured out of them, ghostly tendrils reaching down the halls and shelves as they searched for the book with the answer.

It didn't take long for a dark gray book to fly out of the shelves and into her hand.

The mist retreated back into her eyes, the book opened, and a breeze blew the pages until landing on one in the center.

She looked at Mira, then at me, and then her gaze returned to Ethan's. "To defeat Lilith, you'll need the fourth Holy Object," she said. "The Holy Crown."

"Wow," I said, since the identity of the fourth Holy Object had been one of the questions I'd been contemplating asking. "Where can we find the Holy Crown?"

The mist swirled out of Hecate's eyes again, searching through the Library.

I'd asked a question.

I hadn't meant to ask it. But it had come out so quickly that I hadn't realized it.

Mira's lips were pressed into a firm line.

Ethan's expression betrayed no emotion. Although it was impossible to truly know, since he still wouldn't look at me.

The mist retreated, and a deep red book flew down

the hall, smacking into Hecate's waiting hand. She must have placed the other book down while I'd been lost in my thoughts.

Just like before, the breeze opened the book to a page. Although this time, the page was near the end of the book.

"Hm," she said as she studied the page. As always, she didn't let any of us see what she was reading. "Very interesting."

I bounced on my toes and waited anxiously for her to continue.

"The first place you need to go to find the Holy Crown is in Ember," she said. "To the hidden dragon kingdom. Ethan knows where it is."

Ethan simply nodded.

"I didn't realize the Crown could be in more than one place." I made sure to phrase it as a thought instead of a question.

"Neither did I," she said. "But, you asked where to go to *find* it. Ember is the first place. It's likely that you'll figure the rest out from there."

"You say it like you know it for sure."

"There are many things I know," she said. "And many I don't."

It took all of my effort to stop from rolling my eyes and huffing.

Why were the people with divine knowledge always the most hesitant to share it?

"The journey to Ember is a one-way trip," I said, since I'd learned it in my studies. "Once you enter, you can't leave."

"That's because it's used as a realm for the fae and mages to send their prisoners," Ethan said, scowling. "The spell keeping them there is stronger than any barrier spell in existence. Not even the strongest, darkest supernatural prisoners can figure out to escape. My dad was the only one who could come and go as he pleased. But he never told me how..." Realization flashed over his eyes, and he reached for the chain around his neck.

"What?" Mira asked.

"My dad wore a similar chain around his neck," he said slowly, as if he were trying to recall something he'd learned long ago. "I can't remember what hung from it. But according to Hecate, I have witch blood in my veins. Which means either my father or mother had to have witch blood, too. What if it was my dad? And what if he also had a key?"

"You'd know if your dad wore a key like ours," Mira said. "Right?"

"Except I didn't have a key until recently," he said. "The magic of his key could have stopped me from knowing what it was, or even from remembering it was there."

"Maybe." Mira didn't look convinced. "But you said the spell on Ember is stronger than any other barrier spell. That *no one* can leave once they're there. What if the barrier blocks us from being able to use our keys, too?" She quickly glanced at Hecate. "That question was directed toward Ethan," she clarified. "Not to you."

If Hecate was put off by Mira's snapping at her, she didn't let it show. "I know," she said simply. "Now, what's your question?"

Mira didn't look at either me or Ethan. "Will the keys be able to take us to and back from Ember?"

Hot anger swirled within me. Why did Mira ask her question without consulting us first?

Don't be a hypocrite, I thought. *You asked your question without consulting either of them.*

But my question had slipped out. Which, I supposed, Mira's had, too.

Besides, it was information we needed to know.

"Since I created the keys, I don't need to consult a book to answer your question," Hecate said. "My keys allow to you walk through the door of the Library and into any place you've ever been. This applies to every realm, including Ember."

"But we've never been to Ember," I said. "So we can't use our keys to go there."

"Yes, that's how the keys work," Hecate said.

"So how are we supposed to get there?"

"I'm afraid you've used up your questions for the day," she said.

"Then it's a good thing I know the answer," Ethan said. "Because there are only two portals that lead to Ember. And I'm pretty sure we can get to at least one of them."

8

GEMMA

INSTEAD OF RETURNING to our rooms in the Haven, we went straight to the tearoom.

I picked up the pen and notepad sitting on the coffee table.

Meet us in the tearoom, I wrote. *We have news.*

I ripped the paper of the notepad, folded it, and placed it in my upturned palm.

"There's a witch stationed outside this room," Mira said. "She can send fire messages to Mary."

"I know. But I can't get better without practice."

Every time I'd tried to send a fire message so far, I'd burned the letter with my elemental fire magic instead of sending it to the intended recipient with my witch magic. It was a medium-level spell—Mira still hadn't succeeded with it, either—but our phones wouldn't work outside of the Earth realm. And we needed to be able to communicate no matter where we were. Especially because we had no idea what was in store for us in Ember.

So I was determined to master this spell.

Put an imaginary barrier around your elemental magic, I remembered what Harper had said during our lessons. *Focus only on your witch magic.*

I stared at the paper and recited the incantation.

Magic tingled up from my core, traveled through my arm, and released out of my palm.

A small flame engulfed the letter, then disappeared.

No ashes remained on my palm.

"Yes!" I smiled. "I did it."

"Good job." Ethan nodded with respect. "This will be useful once we get to Ember."

"Thanks." My heart fluttered at the compliment.

Stop it, I told myself. *It was just a compliment. And he didn't even look me in the eyes when saying it.*

I needed to get him alone so I could propose my idea about both of us taking memory potion to forget about that kiss. It would be best for all three of us—me, Ethan, and Mira. Because the kiss never should have happened. And if neither me nor Ethan remembered, it would be like it never *had* happened.

The guilt I was carrying would disappear. Ethan's, too.

I wasn't sure which Haven witch would help us out, but surely Mary could point us in the right direction.

At the thought of Mary, she opened the door and joined us in the tearoom, the letter I'd sent to her in hand. She looked back and forth between me and Mira and held it up. "One of you sent this?" she asked.

"I did." I smiled. "It was my first successful fire message."

"Well done." She walked over to one of the colorful chairs and sat down. "I assume you received an audience with Hecate?"

"We did," I said, and the three of us sat down as well and filled her in on what we'd learned.

She listened attentively, and from her calm expression, I had no idea what was going through her mind.

"There are two realms with portals to Ember," Ethan said. "Mystica and the Otherworld."

Of course, I knew about both realms from my studies. Mystica was the realm of the mages, and the Otherworld was the realm of the fae. The mages of Mystica kept mainly to themselves. But the demons had recently launched an attack on the Otherworld, so now the Otherworld was allied with Earth's supernatural kingdoms. The alliance was new—and apparently very tense and complicated—but at least it was something.

"None of us have ever been to the Otherworld," I continued. "So we can't use our keys to get there. We were hoping—"

"I can't guarantee what kind of reception you'll receive from the fae," Mary said before I could finish the sentence. "But I do have what you need to get to the Otherworld."

9

GEMMA

In all the weeks we'd spent with Ethan since getting our magic, he hadn't told us anything about his home realm. So, for the rest of the day, he prepared us for what to expect when we got to Ember.

At least, he told us what he could, since he'd left Ember when he was a small child. Most everything he knew about his home realm had been told to him by his father.

"We'll take the portal to Ember," he finished. "And then, I'll lead you to the kingdom. Well, what's left of the kingdom." A shadow crossed his eyes at that last part.

"But since you've been there before, you can use your key to go *straight* to your people," Mira said. "You can literally walk in the front door and be there. So why don't you go alone, get the Crown, and bring it back here?"

"Because it's my duty to protect you," he said. "I can't do that from another realm."

"We're safe in the Haven."

"We were supposed to be safe in Utopia, too."

She frowned and said nothing.

"Nowhere is safe," he continued. "But we have our keys. As long as there's a door nearby, we have a way out of whatever situation we find ourselves in."

And what if there's no door nearby?

I kept the thought to myself, since I didn't want to upset Mira.

"Fine," she said, still frowning. "But I'm tired. I'm going to take a nap." She used her key to exit the tearoom—presumably to go to her room.

Ethan watched her leave, his expression hard.

Whatever he was thinking, I couldn't read him. And I didn't know why I thought I'd be able to. He was one of those people who was near impossible to read.

But I could almost always read my twin.

"She wants you to go after her." I motioned at the door.

"She does." He sighed, then looked to me.

My chest tightened. Because this was the moment I'd been waiting for.

Time alone with Ethan to ask him the question that had been on my mind for days.

"Wait." I took a deep breath, glanced down at my feet, and spoke as quickly as possible. "I think we should take memory potion to forget about what happened in that room."

I nearly smacked myself. Could I have been any more generic?

I forced myself to meet his eyes, and he looked… amused.

It was the first time he'd looked me in the eyes in days. My breath caught at the intensity of his stare.

Why did his gaze have so much power over me?

"You mean the kiss?" he asked.

"Yes." My voice nearly got stuck in my throat. "That."

"No."

"What?" I startled.

"You heard me. No. I won't take the potion."

I froze, unsure what to say. In all the times I'd rehearsed this conversation in my mind, I'd never imagined he'd say no—and especially not so quickly.

I shook myself back into focus. "Why not?"

"Because it happened," he said quickly. "And, memory potion or not, we can't change that."

"But we're the only people who know. If we take

memory potion, it'll be like it never happened. And that would be easier—for all three of us."

"What if I don't want to forget?"

Confusion rushed through me. Confusion… and a small thrill of happiness.

No.

I couldn't be happy about this. What we did was wrong. I wouldn't let myself feel anything else.

"We agreed that Mira should never know," I said.

"We did," he agreed. "But just because Mira will never know, it doesn't mean *we* have to never know."

"Why does it matter?" I asked. "It meant nothing. The only reason you snapped out of it was because you thought I was Mira."

"I never thought you were Mira."

"That's not true," I said. "When we kissed, you thought about all the times you'd kissed *Mira*."

"I never said that." His brow furrowed in genuine confusion.

"Yes. You did."

Silence for a few seconds as we stared each other down. Because I knew what had happened. He'd definitely said that he'd flashed back to all the times he'd kissed Mira—to all the memories they'd shared together.

Why claim otherwise?

"Fine," he muttered. "If that's what you want to think to feel better about it, then fine."

"Why are you doing this?" I asked.

"Doing what?"

"Being so… stubborn."

He let out a small chuckle. "You've known me for months," he said. "Haven't you realized? I'm always stubborn."

"You and Mira both," I said.

"And you, too," he said. "You're the most determined, focused person I've ever met. Which, for the record, are nice ways of saying 'stubborn.'"

My breath caught again, and I took a step back to get ahold of myself. "Then you should know that I'm determined to take this memory potion. I have to do it. For Mira."

"You don't have to do anything," he said simply. "But fine. If it makes you happy, take the memory potion."

"So… you'll do it?" That was surprisingly easy.

"*I* won't do it," he said. "But I won't stop you from doing it."

I pressed my lips together. This wasn't getting us anywhere.

"You should get the potion made as quickly as possible," he said, and was it just me, or was there a twinge of pain in his voice? "It takes a few hours to brew, and we're leaving for Ember in the morning."

I stood there, confused. Because why did he want to remember that kiss? It couldn't have meant anything to him.

Could it have?

I nearly asked, but I stopped myself.

"Good point," I said instead. "Thanks."

Without a glance back at him, I spun around, turned my key in the lock, and stepped into the Library's ivory hall.

Hecate wasn't there.

Figured. I sighed in frustration.

Although it was probably a good thing that Hecate wasn't there, because in that particular moment, the only thing I wanted to know was why Ethan didn't want to forget that kiss. And that would be a waste of a question, given that there were so many more important things we needed to know regarding what we were about to face.

I stepped through the door again, and entered Mira's room.

She was lying in bed, staring up at the ceiling while spinning a strand of her hair around her fingers.

She knew I was there, but she didn't move.

I walked over to the bed, laid down next to her, and

also stared at the ceiling. We stayed there like that for a few seconds, in the sort of comfortable silence that only happened with people you'd known your entire life.

"You seem happier," she finally said.

"I do?"

"Yeah. You seem… less burdened. Which makes zero sense, given what we're doing tomorrow."

I let out a long breath and kept staring at the ceiling. Because she was right—it made no sense.

"Maybe I like having a goal again," I said, trying to make sense of it by speaking it out loud. "We were in limbo before, not knowing what to do or where to go. Now, the decision's made. There's nothing else to do but focus on getting it done."

"I guess." She shrugged, and I could tell she didn't relate.

"You want me to sleep in here tonight?" I asked.

"You mean you're finally going to stop avoiding me?"

I sucked in a sharp breath. "What do you mean?"

"You've been avoiding me," she said simply. "It's like you're afraid to talk to me."

"Since when?" Panic filled me. It had to have been since the kiss. She'd noticed.

Of *course* she'd noticed. Mira might not be the most intuitive with magic, but she'd always understood people. Especially me.

"For *weeks*," she said. "Ever since you got poisoned by that nightshade."

"Huh." Something tugged at my thoughts—something important that had happened with the nightshade—but then it was gone. "I'm sorry."

"It's okay," she said. "I know it must have been scary to be that close to death."

"As if we haven't fought for our lives multiple times since getting our magic." I chuckled.

"Tell me about it," she said. "But you know what I mean. I knew we couldn't actually die on Moon Mountain... but seeing you like that... it was awful. There was nothing I could do to help you. I hated it."

"You made the healing potion," I reminded her.

"*Harper* made the healing potion. At least, she did the hard part."

"You started making it," I said. "If you hadn't, Harper might not have been able to finish in time."

"True." She smiled for the first time since I'd come into her room. "Thanks."

"For what?"

"For believing in me."

"I always believe in you," I said. "You're my twin."

"True." She finally moved her gaze away from the ceiling to look at me. "Like it or not, you're stuck with me."

"And I've always got your back," I said. "Just like I will in Ember. We're going to be okay there."

Hopefully the more times I said it, the more I'd believe it.

She nodded, saying nothing. Mira was never one to sugarcoat anything.

"We have a big day tomorrow," I finally said. "We should try to get some rest."

"I don't know if I'll be able to sleep," she said.

"Me, either. But we should try."

I hadn't expected to be able to fall asleep. I hadn't actually wanted to. Because I was going to do what Ethan had suggested and find someone to get me that memory potion. Probably Rosella. She wasn't a witch, but she'd know who to tell me to go to.

But I must have been more tired than I'd realized, because when I opened my eyes and glanced at the clock, it was the next day. Well, the next *night*, because of the Haven's nocturnal schedule.

Mira stretched and rubbed her eyes. "What time is it?" she asked.

Dread pooled in my stomach, and I said, "It's time to leave for Ember."

10

GEMMA

SAYING goodbye to Mom was tough. She tried to be strong, like she'd been when we'd entered into battle with the demons and gone to Lilith's lair. But as strong as she was, she couldn't conceal her worry.

While we couldn't tell her about the keys, since she'd just forget a second later, we calmed her by telling her we could teleport between realms. We said it was an ability that only a rare number of witches had, which was relatively close to the truth.

Eventually, we hugged, said goodbye, and went to the tearoom, where Mary was waiting. Mary was in Haven whites, but the three of us wore brown tunics and pants made from rough cloth that made me feel like I belonged in a medieval village. A witch had procured the clothing for us after Ethan had explained what the people of Ember wore.

Because once we were in Ember, we needed to blend in. That wouldn't be possible in modern clothing or Haven whites.

Mary looked us over. "I was alive when clothing like this was commonplace," she said. "Back then, things were much more... primal."

"Ember is extremely different from Earth," Ethan said. "At least, from present day Earth."

Mary watched me and Mira with worry.

"We'll be okay," I said. "We have Ethan looking out for us."

Ethan nodded, looking pleased with my statement—with my trust in him. There was also a hint of question in his eyes.

He had to be wondering if I'd taken the memory potion.

Would he ask?

No, the answer came to me immediately. Because if he respected my decision, he wouldn't risk telling me and having me find out what I'd done. And I believed he did respect my decision—even though he didn't know what decision I'd made.

Mary walked to the back corner of the room, pressed her hand against the wooden panel, and pushed it open.

A secret door.

"Follow me," she said, and she led us into a dimly lit room hidden behind the tearoom.

A simple fountain—like the ones in the mall people threw pennies into for good luck—took up the majority of the room. Other than that, there were no decorations.

Mary reached into her pocket, pulled out three coins, and handed one to each of us.

I held the coin closer to examine it. Heavier than a regular coin, it was gold, with a portrait of a beautiful, doll-like woman carved into it. A delicate flower wreath sat on her head. I flipped it over and looked at the tall, elaborate crown carved on the back. Letters curved around the crown, spelling out the words "Empress Sorcha."

"Portal tokens," Mary explained. "Together, you'll toss your tokens into the water and jump into the fountain."

Nervous energy rushed through me, and I ran my fingers over the carved surfaces of the coin to calm myself.

"The Empress is waiting for your arrival," she continued. "She doesn't like to be kept waiting."

Ethan stepped up to the edge of the fountain. "We'll hold hands when we jump through," he said. "So we're never in different realms at the same time."

I stared at the water and didn't move. Because we'd be jumping *into* the water and not coming back up.

I hated having my head underwater. Just the thought made my lungs hurt, like they were already begging for air.

How did anyone *enjoy* the sensation of not being able to breathe?

"Gemma?" Mira asked, already standing by Ethan's side. "Are you coming?"

"Of course." I walked up to her side, so Mira was between me and Ethan.

Ethan's jaw tensed.

Had he expected me to stand next to him? Did he *want* me to stand next to him, so he could hold my hand when we jumped into the fountain?

It doesn't matter, I thought, shaking myself out of it. *Even if he wants to hold your hand, it's better for everyone if you don't want to hold his.*

"It'll be okay," Mira assured me. She must have thought I was still thinking about my dislike of the water, instead of beating myself up over my desire to hold her boyfriend's hand.

"I know." I couldn't look at her—or at Ethan. "Let's just get this over with."

Ethan counted to three, and we tossed our coins into the fountain.

Purple mist spread through the water, glittering like a galaxy of stars, and swirled around until it filled the fountain.

"It's time," Mary said. "Go now, before the portal closes."

Ethan and I grabbed Mira's hands at the same time, the three of us stepped up onto the edge, and I barely had time to suck in a deep lungful of air before we jumped into the sparkling purple water.

11

GEMMA

WE DIDN'T MAKE A SPLASH. I didn't even feel my feet hit the surface of the water.

Instead, we floated through nothingness. It was what I imagined it would feel like to float through space.

I opened my eyes, stopped holding my breath, and sucked in cool, crisp air. Bright lines of light surrounded us, and I gazed around in wonder. It looked like the scenes in *Star Wars* when they jumped their ships to light speed.

Before I could glance at Mira and Ethan, my feet hit solid ground, and the racing stars melted away.

I landed with so much force that I fell onto my knees, dragging Mira and Ethan down with me. Luckily, we all reacted in time to let go of each other's hands and catch ourselves with our palms. Otherwise, our faces would have smashed into the marble floor.

The quick reflexes were probably thanks to all that time training with Raven.

There was something under my hand—the gold coin. I grabbed it to place in my pocket, but stopped midway there.

Because there were two pairs of feet in front of us. One in simple, flat sandals, and the other in crystal heels.

I looked up and gasped at the sight of the women standing before us—mainly at their shimmering, iridescent wings that looked like they were made of holographic lines of light.

The woman with the crystal shoes wore a white gown with skirts that puffed out of her waist like Cinderella. Her face was unmistakably the same one as on the coin, and she wore the tall crown from the back of the coin on her pale blonde hair. Her wings were the color of diamonds, and they sparkled just like them.

She had to be the Empress of the Otherworld —Sorcha.

The other woman had gold wings, and she wore a green dress that was far less formal, although its colorful stitching looked intricate and expensive. She watched me with calm gray eyes that held decades of wisdom. Or perhaps centuries, given the immortality of the fae. She stood slightly back from the Empress, as if it weren't clear enough from the Empress's gown and crown that she was the one in charge.

Ethan hurried to his feet. Mira and I did the same.

We were in a large, open-air courtyard with Roman-styled columns lining all four sides of it. The tree leaves and flowers in the gardens were sparse and wilted, like they were barely holding onto life. Perhaps they had trouble getting enough sunlight through the light blue protection dome up ahead—the one that I knew surrounded the entire city.

I refocused on the Empress, who was eyeing Ethan in disapproval.

He bowed his head. "Empress Sorcha," he said.

"King Pendragon," she replied, and then she glanced at me and Mira, waiting.

I did as Mary had instructed us and curtsied. Hopefully the Empress didn't notice my legs shaking. "Your Highness," I said.

Mira curtsied and said the same.

"Gemma," the Empress said to me, and then she looked to my sister. "Mira."

The golden-winged woman gave me a small smile of approval, and I stopped holding my breath.

I hadn't messed up the royal greeting. At least, not terribly enough to cause offense.

"Welcome to the Otherworld," the golden-winged woman said. "I'm the Empress's advisor, Aeliana. We've been expecting you for quite some time."

"But you were only told we were coming yesterday," I said.

"True. However, I've known about your visit for longer than that."

Future sight. It had to be.

Ethan remained focused on the Empress. "Mary said you'd take us to the portal," he said.

"I will," she said. "But as I'm sure Mary also told you, the portal is a one-way trip to the prison world."

"We're aware."

"Very well. Then follow me."

The Empress led us out of the courtyard and up to the roof of the palace. There were marble, Roman-styled buildings on top of it—like a town on top of the roof.

The palace was the tallest point in the city, looking out over the densely packed buildings around it. The buildings closest to the palace were large, sturdy, marble structures. The ones on the outskirts were wood, and they looked like they might topple over at any second.

A few people we passed had wings of a variety of colors and wore stitched clothing like Aeliana. Most had no wings, and they wore gray uniforms that nearly blended into the marble floors and buildings. Red tattoos circled their right biceps, and they kept their gazes down as we passed.

Half-blood servants. The tattoos bound their magic, leaving them at the mercy of the fae.

Selena—the Queen of Wands—was also a half-blood fae. After becoming the Queen of Wands, she'd made a deal with the Empress—an alliance with Avalon in exchange for allowing her to free the half-bloods from their magical chains.

But she'd gotten so caught up in trying to save her best friend Torrence from a goddess that was keeping her captive that she'd yet to return to the Otherworld to free the half-bloods.

According to the witches in Utopia, Selena blamed herself for Torrence getting captured. But Selena was the only person in the world who could use the Holy Wand to free the half-bloods. And as I looked around at the servants we passed—all of them with downturned eyes—I wondered why Selena couldn't have put someone else in charge of rescuing Torrence so she could free the servants she supposedly cared so much about.

I didn't want to dislike someone I'd never met—especially not one of the Holy Queens. But how could Selena leave the half-bloods so helpless when she had the power to free them?

Eventually, we made it to the opposite side of the palace's roof, and the Empress stopped in front of a building that looked like a mausoleum. It was made of marble, and had columns leading to the door.

She reached into a pocket hidden in her skirts and pulled out a black key. She stuck the key into the lock, the key glowed red, like burning coal, and she opened the door.

Aeliana stayed back. "This is as far as I go," she said. "But before you leave, I have something for you." She reached into the satchel tied at her side and pulled out two gold coins.

"More portal tokens?" I said, confused. Because the three of us already had portal tokens. At least, we had the ones we'd borrowed from Mary.

"These are rare portal tokens," Mary said. "They were given to me by the only fae with omniscient sight who'd ever lived—"

"Prince Devyn," I said quickly.

She raised an eyebrow. "You know your history."

"Part of our training after receiving our elemental magic was learning the history of the supernatural world," I explained. "I learned as much as I could."

"Gemma's a great student," Ethan added, and I looked at him quizzically.

Why was he so eager to compliment me?

Mira's lips pinched with annoyance. She never liked when I received praise and she didn't.

I refocused on Aeliana, not wanting to look at Ethan *or* my twin. "Prince Devyn could do more than see the most probable future," I continued. "He could see *all* possible futures."

"Correct." Aeliana nodded. "Which meant he could prepare for more than one possible future. And when he gave these tokens to me, he told me they were the only two portal tokens in existence that connect Ember to the Otherworld. They can be used in any fountain in Ember to create a portal back here. Devyn told me to give them to you before you entered Ember."

"But there are three of us." I reached for the key around my neck, as if getting reassurance that it would work as promised.

Could Hecate have been wrong? And if she had, why were we only getting two tokens instead of three?

"He said the purpose of the tokens would eventually become clear," she said, and she placed them in my hand.

"That's all I know, since I cannot see what will happen to you once you're in Ember. But I wish you the best of luck."

Her expression was grave, like she thought we were dead already.

Mira looked to me, worried, and I could practically read my twin's thoughts.

I'll back out of this if you will.

But we'd already come this far. So I shook my head, thanked Aeliana, and followed Sorcha through the door.

Ethan took Mira's hand and guided her forward.

Of course he did. It seemed like she needed his help with *everything*.

Maybe he liked the fact that she was always scared. Maybe it gave him a higher sense of purpose.

Except when he and Mira had started dating—before we'd gotten our magic—Mira had never been scared of anything.

Realizing I was getting lost in spiraling thoughts, I tore my gaze away from them and refocused on the task at hand.

Inside the mausoleum, a boundary spell the color of Sorcha's diamond wings surrounded a pit of tar. Red glowed out of it, providing the only dim light in the building.

"The portal to Ember," the Empress said. "No one has ever walked through voluntarily."

Ethan stepped forward, not looking scared in the slightest. "There's a first for everything," he said.

His fearlessness amazed me. But of course he wasn't scared. Ember was his home.

I needed to trust that he'd keep us safe there.

I also needed to trust my own ability to keep us safe. Because I had magic, too.

And I wasn't afraid to use it.

12

GEMMA

I'D EXPECTED it to hurt when I jumped through the portal.

It didn't.

Instead, it tingled, like the air was electrically charged.

It wasn't long before I tumbled out and hit the ground, landing directly on my shoulder. Pain shot up it, and I sat up and held it to relieve some of the pressure.

We were in a mostly flat desert with an occasional brown boulder along the ground. It reminded me of the Outback.

Ethan and Mira had been dumped near me. Mira looked frazzled, and Ethan was on his hands and knees, staring at the ground in a daze, like he couldn't stand up.

I didn't have time to ask him if it had started, because

two groups of four people each walked around two giant brown rocks. The group to my left wore long black cloaks with hoods draped over their heads. They were like grim reapers without scythes.

The people in the other group all had wings. Green, red, blue, and yellow. Three of them were men, one was a woman, and they wore gladiator-style warrior outfits with swords strapped to their sides.

The first group was made up of dark mages, and the other was dark fae.

They represented the two major kingdoms in Ember —the Dark Allies. Their alliance was shaky at best, and was held together by one common enemy.

"Dragons." The female fae sneered, looking straight at us.

Mira hurried over to me, her eyes wide with question.

What should we do?

"How did they get loose?" the man next to the female fae said.

She drew her sword. "They don't have cuffs," she said steadily, and the other fae reached for their swords as well. Then she looked back at us and smiled, her red wings the same color as a demon's eyes. "Stay where you are," she said sweetly. "Don't use your magic on us—we won't hurt you unless we need to defend ourselves. You can trust us to keep you safe."

Her voice was calm and musical.

She was putting glamour into her tone.

But we'd been prepared for this. The tiny black stones attached to a thin chain around our ankles protected us from psychic attacks—which included fae glamour.

I stayed as still as possible, hoping it seemed like her glamour had worked on me. Then I glanced at Ethan. He was still on his hands and knees, and he took slow, forced, deep breaths, like he was straining for air.

It was happening.

I nodded at Mira, and she nodded back.

Then the mages reached up and pulled down their cloaks. Two men, and two women. Their eyes swirled with inky blackness, until they were totally dark. Like they had no souls.

"Come with us," the tallest man said. "We don't want to fight. You're more valuable to us alive than dead."

"Why do they get to go with you?" the female fae said. "We'll take the boy—he has the strongest scent. You can have the twins."

"No," the mage said. "We'll take one twin. You can have the other. We'll duel for the boy."

"A duel to the death?"

"A duel until first blood is drawn."

The female fae smirked and tilted her head. "You should take the twins and let us have the boy," she said. "He looks sick."

I squeezed Mira's hand, and we backed away from Ethan to give him space.

It shouldn't be long now...

The mages and the fae continued to watch each other, both groups on guard, apparently unsure how to proceed.

They didn't have time to figure it out, because Ethan's entire body shook with what seemed to be total agony, and then he exploded into dragon form.

He soared up into the air, his red scales glistening in the sunlight, his wings held up regally behind him. I gasped at the sight. Because while I knew dragons were big, I wasn't fully prepared for *how* big. He must have been at least six meters tall, and his wingspan twice that much.

He pulled his head back and breathed a line of fire directly at the leader of the mages.

The mage held his hands up, and black, smoky magic shot out of them, blocking Ethan's fire. The flames mushroomed out around the magic, but Ethan was stronger, and his flames pushed the thick black smoke back down toward the mage.

Then a sword flew through the air like a javelin and sliced through Ethan's right wing.

Ethan roared and pulled back on his magic, barely moving out of the way of the black magic flowing out of the mage's hands. He swung his head around and breathed a line of fire at the fae.

The blaze hit the yellow-winged fae, and he screamed as the fire ravaged his body, consuming his flesh and leaving behind the distinct smell of cooked meat.

Ethan spun back toward the mages and blasted fire at one of them. But like the first mage, she held him off with dark magic.

"We don't want to kill you!" the tall mage screamed up at him. "But we will if we have to."

The fae used this opportunity to lob another sword at Ethan.

He stopped attacking the mage and avoided the sword. Barely.

The fae with blue wings growled, raised his hands, and threw icicles at Ethan.

Ethan blasted the icicles with fire, and they melted before they reached him.

Water magic.

That fae wasn't a normal fae. He was a chosen champion—a half-blood fae chosen by a god to compete in the annual, gladiator-like competition the fae held each year called the Faerie Games. Given his water magic and the blue wings, I assumed he'd been chosen by the god of the sea, Neptune.

But I didn't have much time to think about it, because the tall, male mage shot more dark magic toward Ethan.

I did the first thing that crossed my mind—focused on the rocks surrounding the mage's feet, used my magic to raise them up into the air, and smacked them into the mage's head.

His black magic puffed out, he wobbled, then fell to the ground.

The woman standing next to him kneeled down, checked for his pulse, and let out a pained sob.

I flexed my wrist.

Did I kill him?

It felt like it should've been harder to kill a dark mage.

Hopefully it wasn't, because the other three mages spun to look at me and Mira, their inky eyes swirling with anger.

I cursed and reached for as much magic as possible—both my fire and earth magic.

I'd never taken on a mage. There *were* no mages on Earth to train with.

But there was no time like the present.

"Blast them," I said to Mira, and I blasted them with fire at the same time as my twin shot ice out of her palms.

The female mage—still on the ground—raised one of her hands and held off our elements with a cloud of black smoke. She screamed and pushed harder, and I strained against her magic.

Ethan was also sending fire toward the mages, but he was being held off by the other two.

I glanced to where the fae were standing—except there *were* no more fae standing. Ethan had burned them all to the ground.

But the mage aiming her magic toward me and Mira pushed harder, and I widened my stance, putting everything I had into holding her off with my fire. Mira was now using air, and holding off the other male mage, who'd joined the woman in trying to blast us down.

So much for them wanting to keep us alive. If that smoky magic reached us...

The strongest mages could use dark magic to kill on the spot.

It was closing in on us. And Ethan kept getting closer and closer to the ground.

The swords the fae had thrown into his wings had

ripped through them. And while Ethan healed quickly, he didn't heal *immediately*.

Fear descended upon me.

The mages were beating us.

Not even ten minutes after landing in Ember, and we were failing in our mission. Maybe Mira had been right, and Ethan should have gone without us.

But it wasn't over yet. I needed to try using my earth magic again. Earth magic was trickier, because fire was my strongest affinity, and it was difficult to focus on using more than one element at a time.

Breaking from my fire magic—even for a second—could give the mage the time she needed to overpower me.

But I needed to try. Because what we were doing so far wasn't working.

I needed to reach for more rocks on the ground with my magic, like I'd done to kill that first mage.

I *felt* the rocks at their feet. But trying to raise them was like trying to raise a giant boulder.

"Gemma!" Mira yelled. "She's getting too close!"

Sure enough, there was only about a meter of fire magic between my palm and the black smoke, and she was gaining centimeters on me each second.

Suddenly, red light flashed in the corner of my eye.

Two plumes of dark smoky magic shot out from

where the light had been and smacked into the mages who were attacking me and Mira.

They fell to the ground.

Dead.

The final mage must have been shocked, because Ethan cut through his dark magic and burned him to ash.

I wanted to jump in victory.

Instead, I pulled back on my magic and turned to see where the surprise dark magic had come from, ready to defend myself against whoever had wielded it if they tried to attack us.

Two people.

A girl around my age with long auburn hair, and a guy with jet black hair and skin so pale that I wouldn't have been surprised if he'd grown up underground in Utopia.

Judging from the magic they'd used, they were mages. Dark mages.

So why did they help us?

"Gemma," the girl said, as if we'd met before. "Mira. I take it the dragon is with you?" She motioned to Ethan, and I stared at her blankly.

Ethan lowered himself to the ground. Blood dripped out of the holes in his wings—I had a feeling it wouldn't have been long until he needed to land, anyway—and he shifted back to human form.

He looked exhausted, but his human form wasn't wounded. Thank God.

He hurried over to me and Mira and faced the dark mages. "Who are you?" he asked.

"I'm Torrence," the girl said, then she pointed to the dark-haired guy next to her. "This is Reed. Long story, but we've met the twins before. And we definitely weren't expecting to see you when we landed in Ember."

I stared at her, confused. Because how was Selena's best friend here? And why was she acting like she knew us?

"We haven't met before," I said simply.

"Yes, we have," she said. "Twin Pines Café. We dropped in a few months ago, but you don't remember because we made you forget. Well, *Selena* made you forget."

"The Queen of Wands?" Mira asked.

Torrence's eyes went hard, and she said nothing. Because of course she meant the Queen of Wands.

The Queen of Wands, who was currently on a mission to find Torrence and free her from Circe's island.

If Torrence had been thrown into Ember, and Selena wasn't with her…

"Selena didn't save you," I guessed. "Did she?"

"She tried," Torrence said. "But she shouldn't have. She should have known I could handle myself."

I glanced at Reed. He'd been silent so far, and from his intense expression, I had a feeling he wasn't going to be as open as Torrence.

"Something happened to Selena," Ethan guessed.

"It did." Torrence's voice was flat.

"Did Circe take her?" I asked. "Did Selena offer herself as a trade and take your place on Circe's island?"

It sounded like something one of the Queens would do. Something noble, to save someone they loved.

"Selena's not here because she's dead," Torrence said, her eyes so empty that it put me on edge. "The Supreme Mages killed her."

13

GEMMA

"SELENA HAS the most magic of anyone in the world," I said, shocked. "That's not possible."

"Six Supreme Mages were there," Torrence said. "And they didn't just kill Selena. They killed Selena's soulmate Julian, too."

I shivered at her empty stare. Because Selena was Torrence's best friend. How was Torrence so unemotional right now?

It had to be shock. Selena's death must not have sunk in for her yet.

"Tell us what happened," Ethan said. "From the beginning."

Mira looked around, worried. "Shouldn't we get out of here?" she asked. "What if more of *them* come?" She tilted her head toward the charred remains of the dark mages and fae.

"They rotate the portal guards at nightfall." Ethan glanced up at the sun, which was high in the sky. "We have a while until then. Enough time to hear the two of you out."

I could practically hear the subtext in his tone.

Enough time to figure out if we can trust them.

It seemed crazy to not trust the Queen of Wand's best friend. But there was something *off* about Torrence. Something I couldn't put my finger on.

I barely remembered when she came into the café, but a gut instinct told me she was different than she was then. And if there was anything I'd learned since getting my magic, it was to trust my intuition. It hadn't steered me wrong yet.

"How do you know the guards' schedule?" Mira asked.

"I'm the King of Ember," Ethan said. "There might not be many dragons left, but this is our realm. We know what goes on in it."

She nodded, apparently satisfied with his answer.

I hadn't even thought to question him, because if Ethan thought we were in danger, he never would have suggested staying put.

There were only two people he thought could be putting us in danger right now—Torrence and Reed.

So I turned my attention to them, waiting for them to explain.

"What do you all know?" Torrence asked. "Because the last I'd seen the two of you, you were witches with barely any magic and no knowledge of the supernatural world. Now, you have elemental magic. *Strong* magic, from the looks of it."

"Dragon magic," I said.

"Right. Your mom said you were supposed to get dragon magic on your seventeenth birthday. I guess she was right."

I held up my hand and ignited a flame in my palm. "Dragon magic *is* elemental magic," I said, and I closed my fist, snuffing out the flame.

"Impressive," she said, although she looked anything but impressed.

"We've learned a lot since getting our magic a few months ago," I said. "We were educated on the entire supernatural world. We know you bargained with Circe, lost, and ended up a prisoner on her island."

"For all eternity," Torrence sneered.

"Right," I said. "You made the bargain to help save Selena from the Otherworld when she was held captive there. So, she felt obligated to save you in return. She, Julian, and Reed—" I paused to look at him when I said his name. He stared straight back at me, and I shuffled my feet uneasily, refocused on Torrence, and continued, "They created a search party with the Supreme Mages to find you and save you."

Torrence curled her hands into fists when I mentioned the Supreme Mages, and inky blackness swirled in her eyes.

The same inky blackness that I'd seen in the dark mages. And then, I realized...

"You used mage magic when you helped us fight the dark mages," I said. "But you're not a mage. You're a witch."

"Half-witch," she corrected me. "Half-mage. Apparently, I take after my dad." She paused, then clarified, "He was the mage. Well, he *is* the mage. Apparently he's still alive. And he's here, in Ember."

"That's why you're here?" I asked. "You want to find him?"

"Wait," Ethan said before Torrence could answer. "Let's backtrack a bit." He faced Reed. "How—and when—did you, Selena, Julian, and the Supreme Mages find Aeaea?"

Aeaea—the name of Circe's island. In Utopia, I'd learned that Circe had the ability to *move* the island. It made her nearly impossible to track when she didn't want to be found.

And she hadn't wanted to be found by Selena, Julian, Reed, and the Supreme Mages. That was what had been taking them so long to find the island.

"About two weeks ago, the Supreme Mages used their magic to find the island," Reed said coolly. "We were working on a bargain with Circe. Trying to find something she'd trade in exchange for letting Torrence go."

"How was that working out?" Ethan asked.

"Not well."

"Not surprised."

"We anchored our boat to her island, so that if she moved the island, we'd go with it," Reed continued. "Then, after about two weeks of unsuccessful discussions, Circe's palace exploded like a bomb had gone off. It took out the majority of the island. We were only safe because we were on the edge of it."

"She was trying to blast you out?" I guessed.

"No." Torrence's eyes were now completely black. "I did it. It was how I killed Circe."

"*You* killed Circe? On your own?" I asked, baffled. Because Circe was far more powerful than Torrence. It shouldn't have been possible.

"Circe pissed me off," Torrence said simply. "She pushed me to a breaking point. So I killed her."

Her eyes returned to normal, and they were so haunted that dread filled my body.

"Circe was toying with me." Torrence's voice shook, but she straightened and got ahold of herself. "For weeks, she'd been trying to seduce me. But it wasn't working. She isn't my type." She glanced at Reed, then looked away when she saw he was already looking at her. "Eventually, she got impatient. You wouldn't think an immortal sorceress would get impatient, given all the time she must have on her hands." She chuckled darkly, then continued, "But she did. She tried to force herself on me. And when she did… I exploded." She motioned her hands outward and made a sound like a bomb going off.

"You blew her—and her island—up," I said, and Torrence nodded. "How?"

"I don't know." She shrugged. "But I did. I was the only thing alive on that island after the blast."

I studied her, confused. Because something didn't add up. If Torrence had been there, alive and free on the island, and the rescue party had survived the blast, then why weren't they all safe on Avalon right now?

Why had the Supreme Mages turned on Selena and Julian, and why were Torrence and Reed in Ember?

"Hm." Ethan looked as suspicious as I felt. "What happened after that?"

"Julian, Selena, Reed, and the Supreme Mages found me curled up where the palace had been, covered in ash. And then, the mages sentenced me to Ember."

"What?" I balked. "Why?"

"Because she went dark," Reed said. "Once a mage gives in like that, there's no coming back. All mages who give into darkness are sent to the prison world. Ember."

I waited for Torrence to deny it.

She didn't.

Instead, she smirked. "I didn't only kill Circe," she said. "Because I wasn't the only one she'd trapped there. She kept hundreds of men—men she'd turned into pigs. And when I turned that island to ash, the pigs went, too. All of them. Dead."

"So you murdered hundreds of people," I said darkly.

"Yes. And I don't regret it."

Reed gave us a look as if to say, *See? She's completely dark.*

Torrence stood there, unaffected by her admission.

At least there was one thing clear from her answers so far—she wasn't holding anything back. She felt no guilt for what she'd done. She didn't even seem to care that her best friend was dead.

"What happened to Selena?" I asked. "Why did the Supreme Mages kill her?"

"Right after rescuing me—while still on Circe's island—Selena tried to talk the Supreme Mages out of my sentence," she said. "When they didn't budge, she used her magic on them. Not dark magic—she wasn't trying to overpower them. I think she was just trying to scare them. She'd been working with them for weeks, so she didn't expect them to turn on her. So she was unprepared for all six of them to use dark magic on her at once. The type of dark magic that kills—the type you saw us use here today." She glanced at the dead mages nearby. "She probably could have defended herself with the Holy Wand—if she'd been ready. Then her soulmate —Julian—was so torn up that he also attacked the Supreme Mages. They took care of him *real* quickly."

Chills ran up and down my spine at how calmly she was telling us this.

"And the Holy Wand?" Ethan asked.

"It's gone." Torrence shrugged. "Selena stored it in the ether in the final second."

Ethan's brow furrowed. "What do you mean?"

"Oh, right—you'd have no way of knowing about that. You know that Selena and Julian were gifted with magic from the gods," she said, and I nodded. "Selena received lightning and storm magic from Jupiter, the king of the gods. Julian received fighting magic from the god of war, Mars. One of Julian's abilities was that he could pull any weapon he wanted from the ether—an invisible space between worlds. Selena was able to amplify that ability with the Holy Wand and cast a spell that allows a person to store a weapon they chose in the ether." She reached into the air and pulled a sword out of nowhere. Her eyes glinted with excitement. "Cool, right?"

"Very cool." I nodded, not wanting to say anything that might provoke her to use that sword on me. Or on Mira and Ethan.

Luckily, Torrence pushed the sword back into that same invisible place in the air, like the ether was an invisible locker that was always by her side.

"I tried to use it to attack Circe a few times," she said. "It never worked. She let me keep it—probably because she didn't think I could hurt her with it."

"So the Holy Wand is locked in the ether, and the only person who can remove it—Selena—is dead," Ethan said, as if trying to get it all straight. Torrence nodded, and he continued, "Is there any other way to retrieve the Wand?"

"Not that I know of," Torrence said. "And good riddance to that. You should have seen Selena with that thing. No one should ever have that much power."

Was it just me, or did she sound *jealous?*

"The Supreme Mages followed through on their sentence and threw you into Ember." Ethan remained calm as he spoke—like he was also trying not to set Torrence off. Then he looked to Reed. "Why are you here?"

"I'm not dark, if that's what you're asking," Reed said. "But I love her."

Torrence flinched, but her expression remained stone cold.

"I couldn't let her come here alone," Reed continued. "So I attacked the Supreme Mages. But I'm the firstborn son of a highborn mage, so they wouldn't dare kill me. Instead, they sentenced me to Ember. Just like I wanted them to."

"I told him not to do it," Torrence said. "He didn't listen."

"Damn right I didn't listen."

From the fierce, determined way he looked at her, it was clear he loved her.

Before she'd gone dark, she'd earned this stoic, guarded mage's heart.

Torrence had been through a trauma. But before that, she'd been good. I knew it.

No one is ever purely good or purely evil, Makena's statement from back in the Ward echoed in my mind.

When guided by someone who believes in them, even the darkest souls have the potential to see the light.

Reed loved Torrence. He *believed* in her.

And my intuition told me to believe in her, too.

"You saved us from those mages," I finally said. "What do you want in return?"

"Easy," Torrence said. "I want you to help us get back to Earth."

Us. Not *me.*

She cared about Reed enough to want him to go back with her.

It wasn't much, but it was a start.

"What do you want to do once you're back there?" Ethan asked.

"The witch Lavinia took something from me that I needed." Her eyes swirled with inky blackness again. "Once I'm back on Earth, I'm going to find her. And then, I want to kill her."

Ethan studied Torrence, like he was seeing her in a different light. "As do I," he finally said.

"Good." She smiled. "We're on the same side."

"Apparently so."

I nearly touched my pocket where I'd put the two portal tokens, but stopped myself. No need for Torrence or Reed to ask what I was hiding in there.

"We can help you," Ethan said. "But you were sent

here for a reason. And as much as I'd love to fully trust you, we need to be careful."

Torrence raised an eyebrow. "Are you asking for a blood oath?"

"I am."

"Great." She removed her sword from the ether and examined its sharp edge. "Then let's get started."

14

HARPER

THREE KNOCKS SOUNDED on the door.

I sat on the edge of the twin bed, glared at the door, and said nothing.

The person on the other side opened it anyway.

No, not a person.

A *demon.*

"Food delivery." The demon shoved a quivering human man into the room with me. The man fell down onto his knees. "Drink up."

Then the demon pulled the door shut and locked it, leaving me alone with the human.

My throat burned as I stared at the man, and an ache built in my gums. I barely saw what he looked like. All I could focus on was the pulsing vein on his neck as I inhaled the sweet, tantalizing scent of human blood.

I was so hungry that my bones felt hollow. I had no idea how much time had passed, but I was pretty sure Lavinia had kept me in transition for as long as possible, to torture me with starvation until right before I died from it.

Which explained why I wanted to sink my teeth deep into this human's neck and drink every drop of blood in his body.

But I clenched my fists and held my breath, blocking out the smell of the blood. Then, I moved my gaze away from the human's neck and met his dark brown eyes.

This scrawny, bearded man with deep circles under his tired eyes was a far contrast from the beautiful human men who'd lived in Utopia.

He watched me with resolve, like he was prepared to die.

I can't, I told myself. *I'm going to be a strong vampire. Strong enough to resist the temptation of human blood. My first act as a vampire* won't *be murder.*

Of course, I needed to drink his blood to complete my transition. But I didn't have to kill him. A full meal would suffice. The vampires in Utopia drank anywhere from one to three pints a day. A human could lose about three to four pints of blood before passing out.

If he passed out, I'd know I drank too much.

So I'd have to take it slowly.

Somehow.

"Hold out your wrist." I breathed in the least amount of air as possible as I spoke.

He blinked, confused. "You're not going to kill me?"

"Not if I can help it."

And I *could* help it.

He raised his arm to expose the inner part of his wrist, shaking. The thick vein there pulsed—not as much as the one on his neck—but enough. And I knew from the vampires in Utopia that while drinking blood from the wrist wasn't quite as satisfying as blood from the neck, it was easier to maintain self-control.

"This will probably hurt at first," I said. "Sorry." Not wanting to make this take any longer than necessary, I held my breath again and took slow, measured steps toward him.

He stayed still, apparently smart enough to know that sudden movements wouldn't fare well for him.

I lowered myself down onto my knees, grabbed his wrist, and sank my teeth into the vein.

Sweet, warm blood poured down my throat.

Euphoria.

My breathing quickened as I drank, and I tightened my grip around his arm. His blood flooded through me, and the hunger stopped gnawing my stomach and bones.

How much blood had I had so far? I had no idea. But the more I drank, the stronger I felt.

His arm grew limp.

I cursed and pushed him off me.

He lay on the floor, dazed, but alive.

I licked the remainder of his blood from my lips, watching as the puncture marks on his wrist started to heal. I expected to be hypnotized by the scent of his blood, but while it still smelled delicious, my stomach didn't hollow with pain like it had before.

I'd had enough, and my body knew it.

I backed into the corner of the room and stayed focused on the man, who was lying on his back, relieved tears streaming down his face.

I didn't know what to say to him. Ideally, I'd be able to tell him it would be okay—that I could help him. But he was trapped in Lilith's demon den just like I was.

Even though I hadn't finished him off, I suspected Lilith would send him off to another vampire who would. Of course, that was assuming she kept other vampires in this place. I hadn't seen anything but the room where she'd kept Jamie Stevens, and the room where she was keeping me. Both were small with no windows, so there was no way to know where in the world I was.

I was standing there staring at him when a familiar tingle rose in my core and expanded through my body.

Magic.

Impossible. When witches became vampires, they lost their magic. Whatever I was feeling couldn't be real. It had to be a phantom feeling, like when people lost a limb and felt like it was still there.

But I'd know my magic anywhere…

There was only one way to find out.

I closed my eyes, then teleported from one side of the room to the other.

I was still looking at the man on the ground—but from the opposite direction.

A thrill shot up my body, and it took everything in me not to spin around and cheer with victory.

I still had my magic. And I didn't intend on staying in this cramped, creepy room for a moment longer.

I hurried over to the man, took his hands, closed my eyes, and focused on teleporting to my destination.

Nothing happened.

Of course not. Like most places where supernaturals lived, Lilith had a boundary spell cast around her lair. I could teleport within this room, but I couldn't teleport *out*.

I reached for Hecate's key around my neck. Then, I

looked sadly at the human man nearly passed out on the floor.

Because the keys only worked for their owners.

I wouldn't be able to bring him with me.

But I needed to get out of there. I had no idea what Lilith and Lavinia wanted with me, but they wouldn't have turned me into a vampire for no reason.

I thought back to Jamie Stevens and her red, demon bound eyes…

I refused to let them make me a slave to Lilith. I'd be of no help to *anyone* if that happened. I'd be able to save more people by leaving—even though it meant leaving this human man behind.

I *had* to do it. Because this was war. There were always casualties in war.

"I'm sorry," I said to him, and then I walked over to the door and took a deep breath.

Please don't reject me, I prayed to Hecate, since even though I still had my witch magic, I didn't know if she'd accept me now that I was a vampire.

I steadied myself and stuck my key into the lock. It glowed with magic, and I clicked it open, then stepped into the ivory hall of Hecate's Eternal Library.

The door shut behind me, and I could breathe again.

I was safe.

And I was definitely still a witch.

How?

As I thought it, Hecate walked through the door on the opposite end of the hall. She wore a long purple dress that glimmered like a galaxy of stars. Her long black hair flowed down to her waist, just like mine.

Other than the different eye color, the resemblance between the two of us hadn't passed my notice.

"Harper," Hecate greeted me. "You've changed."

I almost sarcastically said, *You noticed?* But I stopped myself.

No way was that going to be my one question.

"I almost died back there," I told her. "I *would* have died. But Lavinia had me changed into a vampire."

"She did." From the way Hecate spoke, it sounded like she was already aware of my situation.

"I shouldn't be able to use my witch magic," I continued. "I shouldn't still *have* my witch magic."

Hecate said nothing.

And I knew *exactly* what I wanted to ask her.

"Why do I still have my witch magic?"

"Come with me." She spun around and walked toward the doors that led to the never-ending hall of bookshelves. As always, a few people dressed in clothes from different decades wandered around, examining the shelves and occasionally taking a break to grab food or drink from the long banquet table in the center.

I followed Hecate to the podium at the start of the hall.

She stood in front of it, stared forward, and released starry mist from her eyes. It crawled through the hall, tendrils snaking along the shelves and brushing against the blank spines of the books as they searched for the one that held the answer to my question.

It didn't take long before the mist retreated, bringing a book with it. The book landed in Hecate's hands, flipped magically through the pages, and settled on one near the back. Once it did, the goddess's eyes returned to normal.

As she read what was on the page, she held the book at an angle so I couldn't see its contents.

"A book you've seen before," she finally observed.

"Really?" I couldn't believe it, given the endless number of books in the library.

"A list of the most recently turned gifted vampires, with your name at the end. Harper Lane—gifted with the ability to still use her witch magic."

I replayed her words in my mind, and joy rushed through me. "So my magic won't go away?"

"You've already asked your one question," she said.

I rolled my eyes, since obviously I wasn't asking a *question* question—the kind that required her to find a book on the shelves.

"Vampire gifts are permanent," I said instead. "I'll have my gift forever."

And now that I was a vampire, *forever* meant a lot more than it did when I was a witch. Because vampires were immortal.

I was *immortal*. I was going to stay seventeen forever.

The knowledge that I now had endless years ahead of me didn't feel real.

At least I looked mature for my age—easily able to pass as someone in their twenties.

"Are you all right?" Hecate asked.

"Yeah," I said. "It's just… a lot to process."

"It is. Now, I must take my leave. And I recommend you do the same." She glanced at the witches roaming the aisles, as if saying, *You don't want to stay here and end up like them.*

"Wait," I said, and she watched me patiently. "Thank you. For letting me keep my magic."

"I had nothing to do with it," she said. "It was all you. You've always been extremely gifted with magic. And, as you know, when people with an extraordinary ability are turned into vampires, that ability amplifies."

"Of course." I nodded slowly, still in shock that I had my magic. I'd spent days locked in that room while in transition, devastated about losing it.

Now, I had it back.

And I was going to use my gift to get revenge for the destruction of Utopia, by doing everything I could to kill Lilith, Lavinia, and every single demon and dark witch who walked this Earth, until the supernatural world was safe again.

15

HARPER

I USED my key to enter the Haven's tearoom. No one was there.

So I walked to the notepad, picked up the pen next to it, and wrote, *It's Harper. I'm alive and in the tearoom. Get the twins and Ethan, and meet me here.*

I folded up the paper and sent it as a fire message to Mary.

Minutes later, Mary, Rachael, and Raven rushed inside. They stared at me like I was a ghost.

"Where are the twins?" I asked. "And Ethan?"

"You're a vampire," Mary said, as if she hadn't heard my question.

"I am."

"But you just sent a fire message."

"I'm a gifted vampire. My gift is the ability to use witch magic. I'll explain more when the twins and Ethan get here."

"They're not coming," Rachael said flatly.

My stomach twisted, and I braced myself for the worst. "What happened?"

"They've left on a mission to Ember," Mary explained. "Now, I think we should all sit down. I'll send for food and refreshments. Because we have a lot to catch up on."

"Neither of my daughters will go dark," Rachael said for what must have been the fifth time.

"That's what I told Lavinia," I said. "But she sounded pretty convinced otherwise."

"She's wrong."

"I know."

Except there was no way to *really* know. Anyone could go dark if they were pushed to a breaking point. And we had no idea what was happening to them in Ember.

"Someone needs to go to Ember and warn them," I said. "I'll do it."

"No," Mary said sharply.

"Why not?"

"It's too dangerous."

"I'm a vampire gifted with witch magic," I said. "I can handle danger."

"And Ember is a prison realm full of dark mages and dark fae. Yes, you're strong, but they're stronger."

"You don't believe in me."

"I absolutely do believe in you. But this is their mission—not yours. And like you said, you're a vampire gifted with witch magic. That makes you incredibly unique."

"What's the point of being 'incredibly unique' if I can't do something to help?"

"Why do you think you can't do anything to help?" Raven asked.

"Because they're in Ember," I said. "And I'm here."

"I wasn't referring to helping Ethan and the twins," she said. "I'm talking about what's happening here on Earth. You said you want to help us win against the demons. So, figure out what you can do to help us *here*."

I sat back, frustrated. Because ever since Ethan and the twins had arrived in Utopia, I'd been in charge of overseeing their training. Their mission *was* my mission.

But what if it wasn't? Because as much as I hated to admit it, Mary had a point about the danger in going to

Ember alone. And if there was anything I'd learned while in Lilith's lair, it was that I wasn't invincible.

My impulsive actions had nearly cost me my life. I didn't intend to make the same mistake twice.

"Where am I supposed to go?" I asked. "My home is gone."

"You know you always have a home here," Mary said.

"Thank you. But I can't stay here."

She didn't look surprised by my answer. "Why not?"

"Because I want to be the strongest vampire I can be. The only way to do that is by drinking human blood."

Part of the deal of living in the Haven was that the vampires agreed to survive on animal blood. I supposed it was noble of them. But it made them weaker.

And I refused to be weak.

"I understand," Mary said with a kind smile. "And I agree that you likely wouldn't be happy living in the Haven. But the offer is always there."

I sighed, thinking of my home once again. I'd give anything to go back. As a high witch of Utopia, I had a place and purpose there. I had family. I had friends.

Now, I had nothing.

"Why are we bothering debating this?" Raven cut in. "The answer's obvious."

"It is?" I perked up, ready for anything.

"Of course." She smirked. "You're powerful. You're

unique. You want to become the strongest version of yourself, and you want to kill the demons as much as the rest of us. Which means you belong in Avalon, so you can get the best training in the world and join Avalon's Army."

16

GEMMA

We took the horses that had belonged to the dark mages and fae, and set off across the continent.

Thanks to Ethan's knowledge of the land, we didn't encounter anyone on our journey. Ember was mainly desert—not very hospitable to life—so the Dark Allies didn't roam far from their kingdoms. And the dragon kingdom wasn't far from the portal—only a day and a night by horse, with the horses going as quickly as possible.

Eventually, we rode so far that we reached the ocean.

Ethan stopped his horse in a cove that reminded me of my cove at home. "We're here," he said.

I looked around, confused. Ethan hadn't told us much about the dragon kingdom, in case we encountered any issues along the way. Meaning, in case any of us got taken by the dark mages or fae. He couldn't risk the Dark Allies discovering the dragon kingdom's location.

"There's nothing here," Mira said.

"Which is exactly what the Dark Allies think." He jumped off his horse and led it toward the entrance to a cave carved into the cliff. "And what we want them to believe."

We followed him inside, only having to walk about half a kilometer before reaching a pool of water. The inside of the cave would have been pitch black to humans, but thanks to our supernatural vision, it was like walking outside on a night when the moon wasn't shining. Dark, but doable.

Ethan stopped near the water and tied his horse to a rock. "Here's the entrance."

The cave didn't continue farther.

My attention went back to the water, and my chest tightened. "You're not saying..." I trailed off, unable to say it out loud.

"The dragon kingdom is underwater." Mira apparently had the same thought as me.

"Yes," Ethan said.

"How far underwater?" I asked.

"About three kilometers."

I stepped back until my palms pressed against the

cave wall. The warm energy of the solid rock calmed my racing heart, helping me think clearly.

"How are we supposed to get down there?" I asked.

"We have powerful water elementals who keep watch through the water. They're able to watch the entrance of the pool as if gazing through a looking glass," Ethan explained. "They can hear through the water, too."

"Cool," Mira said. "I want to learn how to do that."

"It's advanced water magic. But I'm sure you'll master it in time."

She smiled at his belief in her.

"So they'll be able to hear us," I said. "Then what?"

"They'll send water elementals to get us," he said. "It'll be fine. You'll see."

I watched the water warily. I had no doubt we'd survive, but I couldn't imagine the journey down *kilometers* of water as being anything but terrifying. All of that water closing in around us, ready to drown us at any moment…

I shuddered at the thought of it.

This must have been what Mira felt like when we were in the underground kingdoms.

And we weren't even down there yet.

"What about thc horses?" I asked.

"Water elementals will come up and bring them to a location far enough away that if the Dark Allies stumble across them, they won't be able to track them back here," he said. "From there, the water elementals will shift and fly back home. We're far enough away from both of the dark kingdoms that they won't be spotted."

"You've really got the hang of all this," Torrence said.

"The Dark Allies have lived in Ember for centuries," he replied. "During that time, we've learned how to stay safe and hidden. There wouldn't be any of us left otherwise."

She made a noise of what sounded like approval.

Ethan kneeled down next to the still water and dipped his finger into it. Ripples traveled outward.

Seconds later, an older woman's face appeared in the water. There was light behind her, and her features were decently clear—it was like we were looking in on her through old, foggy glass.

She studied Ethan, and her eyes widened. "Prince Pendragon?" she asked.

Ethan's expression turned solemn. "It's King Pendragon now."

The woman turned her eyes down and muttered a prayer. Then she refocused on Ethan. "I'll send an envoy for you immediately. How many are traveling with you?"

"There are four others," he said. "And five horses."

"Understood," she said. "Welcome home, and we'll see you soon."

Ten water elementals—five males, and five females—surfaced about ten minutes after Ethan spoke to Galinda. That was the name of the older woman who'd appeared to us in the water. He'd known her as a kid while living on Ember, which was how she'd recognized him.

Galinda wasn't in the envoy sent for us. All ten of the water elementals appeared to be in their twenties, or early thirties at the most.

They kneeled to Ethan after surfacing, with sadness in their eyes. "King Pendragon," they said, mostly in tandem.

"Rise," Ethan said, and they did as he commanded.

It was strange to see him treated this way, especially by people older than him. Back at home, he'd been just another guy around town. In Utopia, he'd been treated as less than even the human males. In the Haven, he was an equal.

Here, he was king.

It hadn't truly hit me until that moment.

A dark-haired woman glared at Torrence and Reed. "Who are they?" she asked.

"They're mages," Ethan said simply.

"Dark mages." Icicles formed in her hands, ready to attack.

He stepped in front of her and stared her down. "They're with us."

"They're our enemies."

"Are you questioning your king?"

She held his gaze, then backed down. "Of course not. But hopefully you understand my hesitation."

"I do." He nodded.

"I assume this has to do with the two of them." She motioned to me and Mira.

"The Dragon Twins of prophecy?" Ethan smirked.

"I thought that might be the case."

"It is," he said. "And we're wasting time standing here. We need to get down to the kingdom. Now."

"Very well," she said. "Who's first?"

Mira stepped forward. "I am."

The dark-haired dragon studied her in approval. "You'll go with Topher," she said, and a blond, male dragon stepped forward from the side. His hair was the same color as Mira's.

"I'm going to shift," he said kindly. "Then you'll hop on my back, and I'll swim us to the kingdom. You don't have to do anything but enjoy the ride." He waggled his eyebrows at the last part.

"Don't get any ideas." Mira glanced at Ethan and smiled. "I'm taken."

Ethan didn't look back over at her. In fact, Ethan had been quieter than usual since getting to Ember. He hadn't said much of anything to any of us during the journey to the cave.

Topher glanced at me, but I was already avoiding his gaze.

Every time Mira told a guy she was taken, their instinct was to move onto flirting with me. As if since we were twins, we were interchangeable.

It was tiresome, but I was so used to it that I was prepared.

Within seconds, Topher shifted into dragon form. His dragon was a bit smaller than Ethan's, and his scales a deep blue that shined like gemstones. He lowered himself down to the ground, and Mira easily climbed onto his back.

She situated herself, and then he dove into the water so smoothly that there was barely a splash.

I stared at the water with dread.

I did *not* want to do that.

"Gemma?" Ethan said my name softly, his eyes understanding and kind. "How about you go next, so you can get it over with?"

"Sure," I said, since he was right—it was best to get it over with. "Sounds good."

It sounded terrifying.

A girl with curly red hair stepped forward. "Let me guess," she said. "You're a fire elemental?" Her voice was bubbly and sweet, and I liked her already.

"And earth," I said.

"That explains it," she said. "I'm mainly water, but I have some fire in me, too. And I'd be honored to take one of the twins of prophecy to our kingdom. You'll be safe with me—I promise."

"What's your name?" I asked.

"Farrah."

"All right, Farrah," I said. "Let's do this."

Farrah's dragon form was mostly blue like Topher's, but with specks of orange scattered throughout. She was a bit smaller—it seemed like a shifter's dragon form was in ratio to their human form. She showed her razor-sharp teeth in what I assumed was an attempt at a smile and lowered herself down so I could get on.

Climbing onto her back was easy. And judging by the large spike protruding out of the bottom of her neck—right in front of the place where I sat—dragons were meant to have human riders.

I wrapped my hands around the spike, and without warning, she dove into the water.

I sucked in a breath, closed my eyes, and braced myself for the cold.

But there was nothing. No water against my skin.

Slowly, I opened my eyes.

I was still on Farrah's back. We were underwater, inside a giant air bubble. The bubble followed us as she flapped her wings, flying us through the water. It was so dark that I could barely see anything except the outlines of the fish around us.

Then, an orange light glowed in the distance. As we approached, the light grew bigger, until I could make out an entire city at the bottom of the ocean. A domed kingdom with a tall palace in the center and gradually smaller buildings spreading outward into a circle, like the lost city of Atlantis.

"Wow," I said, and Farrah flew through the water faster as we completed our approach.

We reached the dome, and she flew straight through it. The transition between being inside the air bubble around us to being inside the dome was seamless. Not even a single drop of water touched me.

People walking below paused to stare up at us. The streets were lined with blazing torches, which was why the city glowed orange. Fiery light came out of the windows, too.

We flew to the top of the central tower. There was a landing pad on the top of it—like the ones used for helicopters—and Farrah lowered us onto it.

I climbed off her back, and she shifted into human form.

"Where's Mira?" I asked.

"Down below," she said, and I noticed the start of a circular stairway at the corner of the roof. "Where our Elders are waiting to meet you."

17

GEMMA

I FOLLOWED Farrah down to the top floor of the tower, where Mira, Topher, and two others—an older man and woman—were waiting. Despite their silvery hair and wrinkles around their eyes, they didn't look weak.

The high ceilinged, circular room was gothic in design, with dark stone walls and floors. Tall windows looked out of all parts of it to the city below, and guards stood silently between them. The city radiated orange light, and the water surrounding the dome glowed blue. Colorful, reptilian fishes swam outside the dome, like a reversed aquarium, with them looking in on us.

My chest tightened at the thought of all the tons of water pressing down on the dome.

"How was the ride?" Mira asked casually.

"Good," I said. "You?"

"Amazing."

Torrence and her dragon came down the steps next, followed by Reed, and lastly, Ethan.

The Elders dropped down to their knees when Ethan entered.

"King Pendragon," they said in unison.

"Darius," Ethan said to the man, and then he looked to the woman. "Hypatia. It's good to see you again."

"I wish it were under better circumstances," Hypatia said as she and Darius stood back up. "But it's good to see you, too."

Ethan simply nodded in response.

Darius, Hypatia, and all the guards watched Torrence and Reed, on high alert.

"I respect your authority as king," Darius said tightly. "But I expect you have an explanation for bringing two mages into our kingdom."

"I do," Ethan said, and he told them everything that had happened since we'd arrived in Ember.

"They'll be guarded at all times," Hypatia said once he finished. "And we won't hesitate to use force against them if they try anything against us."

"You don't have to talk about us like we're not here," Torrence said. "We can hear you."

"We will talk as we please," Hypatia snapped. "The

two of you may have strong magic, but you're outnumbered here. Don't forget your place."

"You mean we shouldn't forget that we're miles under the ocean, in a kingdom full of dragons who want to kill us?" Sarcasm dripped from Torrence's tone.

Hypatia didn't bother with a reply. Instead, she focused on me and Mira.

"The twins of prophecy," she said warmly, sounding completely different than she had when she'd spoken to Torrence. "The ones who will free our people from their bondage."

The pressure that I already felt from being surrounded by water grew, and I shuffled my feet, nervous. "That's what we've been told," I said. "And we're happy to help in any way we can. But we're not full dragons. We have elemental magic, but we can't shift."

"They also have witch magic," Ethan added.

"A bit," I said.

"Interesting." Hypatia studied us and pursed her lips. "I wonder..." She glanced out one of the windows, then looked to the guard standing closest to the door. "Bring Janelle up to join us," she said. "It's time to see if the twins are the solution we've been waiting for."

18

GEMMA

THE GUARD BROUGHT UP A TALL, middle-aged woman with long, thick, platinum hair. She was nearly as tall as Ethan—she looked like a warrior princess. Her eyes were sharp and intelligent, but there were shadows underneath them.

She was exhausted.

And around her wrists were matching black cuffs.

I'd seen cuffs like those before.

Isobel—the witch Harper had delivered as a prisoner to the Ward—had worn them. They'd stopped her from performing magic.

"Twenty years ago, Janelle and three others were rescued from the Dark Mage kingdom," Hypatia said. "It's the only rescue mission of our generation that's been successfully completed. But, just as the dragons before them who've been enslaved by the Dark Allies, we're unable to remove the cuffs that bind their magic. As long as the cuffs remain on their wrists, they're unable to shift or use their elemental magic."

"They say you can set me free." Janelle held up her wrists, her sharp gaze on me and Mira. "Want to have a go?"

"I don't know if we can," I said, and I looked to my twin. "But we can try."

"How?" Mira asked.

"With our intuition. Let's touch the cuffs and see what we can do."

Mira looked doubtful.

"Those cuffs were created by a Supreme Mage," Reed said simply. "You can't dismantle them."

"They're the dragon twins," Janelle said. "Of course they can dismantle them."

"Let them try." Reed shrugged. "It won't work."

Janelle glared at him, then faced me and Mira. "Come on," she said. "Prove him wrong."

All eyes were on us, and more pressure mounted in my chest. I couldn't look at any of them. All I could do was focus on the cuffs around Janelle's wrists.

How were we supposed to do this? There wasn't a spell like this in any of the books Mira and I had studied. There'd been no mention of magic binding cuffs at all.

"You *can* do it," Janelle said, although she didn't sound as confident as before. "Right?"

"We'll do our best."

I gave Mira a look that said, *you better try your best,* then stepped forward until I was standing in front of Janelle.

Mira joined me. She wouldn't meet Janelle's eyes. She wouldn't meet my eyes, either.

"I'll take one cuff," I told my twin. "You take the other."

I placed my fingers on the cuff closest to me, and Mira did the same with hers. The cuff hummed with magic, although the magic felt dark and draining. Like it was trying to suck out my soul.

No wonder Janelle looked so exhausted.

"I'll follow your lead," Mira told me.

"All right." I closed my eyes and cleared my mind.

Hecate, I thought, and I pictured the goddess, imagining she was there with me. *Guide me on what I need to do.*

I waited for something to click.

Nothing happened.

Silence hung heavy in the room.

"Gemma?" Mira asked, and I opened my eyes. My twin watched me, waiting.

"Focusing on neutralizing the magic." I hoped I sounded more confident than I felt. Because I'd totally made that up. "Draw it out of the cuffs."

"Okay."

I closed my eyes again, and pictured the magic flowing out of the cuffs and into my body.

Nothing happened. So I pulled at it harder.

Still, nothing.

"It's not working," Janelle said, her voice flat. Defeated.

I opened my eyes and took my fingers off the cuffs. Mira did the same.

"I'm sorry," I said. "I *want* to help. I promise I'll figure it out."

"How?"

My hand went to the key around my neck.

Add this to the ever-growing list of questions I had for Hecate. I needed to write down the questions sometime. List them in order of importance. Otherwise, I was never going to be able to keep track.

"I know someone who can help," I said. "I can't say any more than that, but I need you to trust me." I glanced at Mira, then at Ethan. "To trust *us*."

Hypatia watched me curiously. "Who's this 'someone?'" she asked.

"Someone who has answers—to everything."

"Hm." She pursed her lips, studying me. "When will you be able to get these answers?"

"I don't know," I said. "But I'll do my best to get them as soon as I can."

"You do that," she said. "Once you do, you know where to find us."

We all watched each other warily.

The Elders were losing their belief in us.

"We *will* help the enslaved dragons," Ethan said confidently. "You have my word, as your king. But unfortunately, we can't stay here for long."

"You brought the twins here safely," Darius said. "You returned to the kingdom you're destined to rule. Where else do you need to be?"

"We need to return to Earth."

"Now?"

"As soon as possible. As you know, demons threaten their realm. The supernaturals there are fighting, but they're losing."

"What does this have to do with us?" he asked.

"There's something here we've come to get—something we believe can turn the war in our favor," Ethan said.

"*Our* favor?" Hypatia raised an eyebrow. "You speak as if you're one of them, and not one of us."

"Our interests align with the supernaturals on Earth," he said, unfazed by Hypatia's doubt. "Like I said, there's something here we've come to retrieve. This object could be the key in beating the demons. But more than that—if freed, the dragons can help the supernaturals on Earth defeat the demons. We're stronger than any of their species. If we join them, their army will be nearly unstoppable. So it's in their interest to help us free our people—if we agree to help them in return."

"You're proposing an alliance with the supernaturals on Earth," Darius said.

"Precisely. And they'll be more likely to hear us out if we bring this object back to them."

"And what object is that?"

Ethan braced himself, held his gaze with Darius's, and said, "We're here for the Holy Crown."

19

GEMMA

"I'M afraid I can only halfway help you," Darius said.

"What do you mean?" I asked.

"Come with me and I'll show you." He glanced at Torrence and Reed. "The mages will stay here."

"The mages will come with us," Ethan said.

"You don't trust us with them?" Hypatia asked, and from her tone, it was clear that we *shouldn't* trust her with the mages.

She'd probably bring them to a torture cell, like the ones in the Ward.

"Quite frankly, no," Ethan said. "And I don't blame you for that. But I promised them that I'd do everything I could to get them back to Earth, and I intend to stand by that promise. So, they stay with us, wherever we go."

"As you wish." She sighed. "You are, after all, our king."

She didn't sound happy about it.

Darius led us to a lift that reminded me of the ones in Utopia and took it to the lowest possible floor—the basement.

We stepped out into a small room with stone walls, a sand floor, and a single steel door.

Darius removed a skeleton key from his robes and used it to open the door.

It swung open, revealing a huge room full of gold, gems, crystals, and more, in piles up to the ceiling and spilling out everywhere possible. It was like stepping into the Cave of Wonders.

"Are these all magical objects?" I asked, looking around in amazement.

"Mostly, no," Darius said. "They're treasures, but they're not magical. You see, dragons love beautiful objects. We keep them here and gift them to citizens who earn them. A reward system, per se. It gives everyone something to focus on—something bright and shiny to look forward to in such dark times."

"You're hoarding worthless treasure in your basement," Torrence said, like it was the most ridiculous thing she'd ever heard.

"These treasures are our currency. They ensure that everyone does their best to contribute to the kingdom. But not all of the objects here are non-magical." He spun around and led the way through the vault, meandering around the piles of treasure overflowing onto the path.

We followed him, and I *definitely* spotted Torrence eying up some of the bracelets. Mira, too.

Then I spotted a gold pen inlaid with rubies, and slowed down to stare at it. I'd *love* to write in my journal with that pen...

"Dragons," Reed muttered from behind us, and I quickened my pace.

Darius eventually stopped in front of a small, unremarkable wooden box with a tiny keyhole in the front. "Here we are," he said, and then he kneeled down, removed a tiny key from his robes, and opened the box.

Inside were clear crystals about the size of my pinkie finger, tied together at the bottom with wires of gold, in the shape of a half circle. At the end was a taller crystal and half a crescent moon, sawed off in the center.

"Half of the Holy Crown," I realized, and Darius nodded. "Why only half?"

"I don't know," he said. "But we've kept it safe here for centuries. Waiting to give it to you."

Mira's eyes were as wide as they'd been when she

was looking at the bracelets, and she stepped forward to take the Crown.

Darius handed it to her, and I frowned at the fact that Mira got to hold it first.

She gasped as she took in its beauty, and her skin looked more radiant than ever. Her hair looked shinier, too.

It was like the Crown's light had rubbed off on her.

"Wow," she said. "What does it do?"

"No one knows," Darius said. "We thought you could tell us."

Another question to add to the list of things to ask Hecate. I was seriously going to lose track.

"We don't know yet," I said. "But we're going to find out." I reached for the Crown, prepared to pull it out of Mira's hands.

She grudgingly handed it over.

The moment I touched it, I was flooded with warmth. With *magic*. It was like a golden glow came out of the Crown and flowed through me. Pure, light, holy magic that filled me to the core.

"How do we know it's real?" Torrence asked.

"It's real," I said.

"How do you know?"

"Because I can *feel* it."

Before I realized what was happening, Torrence

reached forward and wrapped her hand around the big crystal at the end of the Crown.

Ice rushed through my veins.

And Torrence fell to her knees, crumpled into herself, and cried.

20

TORRENCE

AGONIZING PAIN HIT me so hard that it knocked me over, like I'd been run over by a truck.

Selena was dead.

Julian was dead.

All of those hundreds of men who Circe had turned into pigs on the island were dead.

The only person I was happy to see dead was Circe.

Selena had risked her life to save me. Just like I'd risked my life to save her after the fae had taken her to the Otherworld. She'd trusted the Supreme Mages to help her find and free me.

But she was dead. I was never going to see my best friend again.

Because the Supreme Mages had *killed* her.

They were going to pay for this.

I needed to get to Avalon. Because Selena's parents—the leaders of Avalon—needed to know what had happened to their daughter.

And then it was going to be war against the mages.

But the need for revenge didn't cloud my grief. My heart ached with it. Selena was more than a best friend—she was like a sister to me. With her gone, I'd never feel whole again. A piece of my heart was gone forever.

Someone kneeled down next to me and wrapped his arms around me.

Reed.

I leaned into him, feeling more grounded with him holding me.

"Torrence?" He spoke my name like a question.

With eyes full of tears, I looked up into his dark, concerned gaze.

My heart burst with emotion.

I love you, I remembered him telling me, right before the mages had thrown us down the portal to Ember.

At the time, I'd felt nothing.

Now, love for him crashed over me like a tsunami.

"Reed." My voice cracked when I said his name. "I'm so, so sorry."

"You're back," he said quietly, like he was afraid to get his hopes up.

"I am. And I love you, too. More than you could ever possibly know."

His lips crashed down on mine, and I kissed him back like he was the only thing in the world keeping me alive. He tasted familiar and sweet, and I wished I could take back the pain I'd seen in his eyes ever since he found me on Circe's island. The pain I'd put there—by going dark.

Then, someone cleared his throat behind us.

Darius.

I pulled away from Reed, and we both stood quickly.

Darius watched us like a disapproving grandfather, and heat rose to my cheeks. But I kept a hand firmly in Reed's, and he held mine tightly back, like he never wanted to let go.

"Do either one of you want to explain what just happened?" Darius asked.

"I went dark," I said, although the words didn't feel real as I spoke them. The whole experience didn't feel real—I remembered it clearly, but it was like watching a movie instead of having truly lived it. I recalled everything that had happened, but not the emotions I'd experienced *while* it had happened. "The mages were right to send me to Ember. I was totally and completely dark. But now... I'm back."

"It shouldn't be possible..." Reed looked mystified. "No mage has ever come back after going dark."

Gemma held up the half of the Crown. "It happened after you touched this," she said.

There was something different about her. She looked harsher. Stronger. There was a hardness in her eyes that hadn't been there before.

Or maybe I'd been looking at her differently when I'd been dark. Maybe everyone had looked different then. Softer.

Then I glanced at Mira, and she looked the same as before. Hesitant and a bit scared, like she was uncomfortable in her own skin.

It was a miracle she'd survived that fight with the dark mages and dark fae.

They only survived because I helped them, I thought, although of course I didn't say it out loud.

They'd only gotten their magic a few weeks ago. They were new to it, so what they'd done was downright impressive. And I had faith they'd grow stronger from here.

I believed in them, just like I'd always believed in Selena.

Grief hollowed my heart at the thought of my best friend, and I leaned into Reed for support.

It didn't seem possible that I'd never see Selena again.

But I'd watched her die.

She was gone. Forever. And a part of my soul had died with her. I hadn't realized it then, but I felt it now.

"Touching the Crown brought you back," Reed realized. "The Crown's the key. If we can bring it to the dark mages, we can bring them *all* back."

"Assuming they want to be brought back," Mira said.

"They don't." I remembered the calmness that came with feeling no emotions. The feeling of control—of being unstoppable. Of having what felt like unlimited power and no qualms about what to do with it. "Once they figure out what it does, they'll kill you before you come close to them with it."

"We don't have time to strategize about how to turn an entire kingdom of dark mages good again right now," Gemma said harshly. "Let alone to organize ourselves to execute a plan—*if* we're able to come up with a feasible one that won't get us killed."

Ethan stepped back, like she'd slapped him. "If we can free the mages from the darkness, they might be willing to set the dragons free," he said. "How can we not *have time* for that?"

"Because this is only half the Crown." She spoke slowly, like she was talking to a child. "We need the rest of it. That's our mission, and it has to be our priority. Because if only half of the Crown can do this, imagine what'll happen when it's whole."

Ethan stood completely still, and I had a feeling he was going to fight her.

"She's right," Mira jumped in before he could. "Our mission is to find the Crown. Not *half* of the Crown. The *full* Crown. We have to stay focused on that."

"It's our best hope at defeating the demons." Gemma spoke immediately after her sister, like she was finishing her twin's thought. "It's our best hope at staying *safe*."

That final word snapped Ethan out of his anger. "Right," he said. "You're right. I just hate leaving them there when we have a way to save them."

"Our people have been enslaved by the Dark Allies for centuries," Darius said. "We can survive in their kingdoms for a few more weeks, or months, or even years. We have to think long term. And your plan about allying with the supernaturals on Earth is a good one. With them on our side—*and* with the full Crown, assuming you find the second half of it—we have the best chance of beating the Dark Allies and setting our people free."

21

HARPER

To get to Avalon, you needed to complete the island's entrance Trials.

Only one vampire kingdom could take you to the place where the Trials began—the Vale, which was located deep in the Canadian Rocky Mountains.

So, Mary sent a fire message to the ruler of the Vale, King Alexander. He quickly replied, saying a witch would meet me outside the entrance of the boundary dome.

Like all witches who'd grown up in one of the six kingdoms, I knew the entrance locations to the boundary domes of each one of them. It was part of our training. So I said my goodbyes and teleported out of the Haven, ready for whatever adventure awaited me next.

As promised, a witch waited for me outside the Vale.

Even though I'd been there before, the snowy kingdom built into the enormous mountain stunned me with its beauty. It was a winter wonderland that belonged in a giant snow globe.

"Come with me." The witch didn't bother with an introduction before teleporting me to the throne room inside the kingdom.

King Alexander—a pale skinned, dark-haired vampire—sat on the tallest throne. He looked intimidating, but then he smiled, and his smile was so warm and welcoming that it immediately put me at ease. His wife, Queen Deidre, sat on the throne next to his. They both wore formalwear and had golden crowns upon their heads.

A vampire with warm brown skin, dark hair, and bright blue eyes stood next to the king. He wore jeans and a button-down shirt, and he was startlingly attractive. He could have easily passed as a Bollywood movie star.

Who is *he...?*

"Harper," King Alexander said, and I turned my focus back to him. "Welcome to the Vale. Although, from your letter, it sounds like you won't be here for long."

"I've come to enter the Angel Trials," I said proudly.

"I'm sure the Earth Angel will be delighted to have you on Avalon."

As King Alexander spoke, my eyes strayed to the bright blue ones of the vampire next to him.

The corner of his lips turned up in a devious smile, and I lowered my gaze as heat flooded my cheeks.

Why was he watching me like I amused him so much?

"Harper." Queen Deidre snapped me back to attention. "Might I introduce you to our brother, Prince Rohan?" She motioned to the blue-eyed vampire, who still watched me with amusement. "He'll be escorting you to the location where you'll begin the Angel Trials."

"Your Highness," I said with a polite nod.

"Call me Rohan." His voice was smooth, like silk.

I was so hypnotized by everything about him that I nearly forgot to smile.

Come on, Harper, I told myself, shaking myself out of it. *You never get this worked up about a man. Especially one you're never going to see again.*

To make it worse, he was a *vampire.*

In Utopia, we were taught that male supernaturals were naturally power hungry—that they weren't to be trusted. We were supposed to be repulsed by all of them, or at least constantly on guard around them.

So why did Rohan's eyes make me feel like they were calling every cell in my body to come closer to him?

If I wasn't wearing an onyx ring, I would have sworn he was using compulsion on me.

He was so flawlessly good-looking that he had to know it. How many vampire—and human—women in the Vale had he swept off their feet, gotten to fall head over heels for him, and left heartbroken at the end of it? Probably countless amounts.

No way was I letting myself be alone with him. Nothing good could come from it.

I got ahold of myself and looked to Queen Deidre. "I'm sure you're aware of our beliefs and customs in Utopia." I swallowed away a small lump in my throat as I spoke of my destroyed home. "I think it would be most appropriate for you to lead me to the starting point of the Angel Trials. Or at least another woman who knows its location."

Rohan smirked and crossed his arms over his chest. "Afraid to be alone with me?" he asked.

"I'm not *afraid*." Annoyance stirred in me at how cocky he sounded.

"It sure sounds like you are."

Queen Deidre's gaze bounced back and forth between the two of us like she was watching a tennis match.

"I'm surprised," Rohan continued before I could respond. "From what I've heard, you're a vampire gifted with the ability to use witch magic. Surely I should be the one afraid of you?"

I raised an eyebrow in challenge. "*Are* you afraid of me?" I asked.

"I'm not."

"Maybe you should be." The words were out of my mouth before I realized they could be construed as a threat.

Threatening a royal of a vampire kingdom while you were a guest in said kingdom was never a good idea.

"Not like I would ever hurt you," I quickly covered up my mistake. "As long as you don't do anything to warrant it."

"I'd never dream of hurting you," he said, and I sucked in a sharp breath at how sincere he sounded.

Neither of us spoke for a few seconds. We just stared at each other, not wanting to be the one to look away first.

Had he left me speechless?

Queen Elizabeth would be ashamed if she saw me now. My mother would be, too.

But there was something about Rohan...

"I promise that my brother is no threat to you," Queen Deidre said. "But if you prefer me to escort you to the start of the Angel Trials, then I'm more than happy to grant your request."

Rohan watched me, challenging me.

After what he'd just said to me, I'd seem weak if I accepted the queen's offer—even though I was the one who'd asked her to be my escort.

But having the queen accompany me would be far more appropriate than going alone with Rohan.

Screw what's more appropriate, I thought. *What do* I *want?*

"Thank you for the offer," I said to the queen. "But I'll go with Rohan."

22

HARPER

Rohan led me down a huge hall more decadent than anything I'd ever seen. It was so beautiful that I wanted to slow down to take it all in.

"You coming?" he asked over his shoulder.

"Sorry." I hurried to keep up, although I kept looking around as much as possible as we walked.

"The palace is French in design," he explained, like he was giving me a tour. "This specific hall was inspired by the Hall of Mirrors in Versailles."

"Interesting." I nodded as if I knew what he was talking about.

He smiled, like he could tell I'd never heard of the Hall of Mirrors, but he didn't call me out on it. Instead, he slowed down and walked at my pace as I took in the beauty of the palace.

Eventually, he turned a corner into a smaller hall and stopped at a plain wooden door at the end of it. The door was the most unremarkable thing I'd seen in the palace so far. It looked positively medieval.

"This is the start of the Angel Trials?" I asked.

"You think we'd make it that easy?"

"No," I said, since when was anything in the supernatural world ever easy? "Of course not."

He took an iron key out of his pocket and unlocked the door, revealing a stone staircase that circled downward. Torches lined the walls to light the way. The path was so narrow that we'd have to walk single file.

"Follow me," he said, and he started down the stairs.

I followed, and jumped as the door shut loudly behind me.

"You spook easily?" he asked.

"No." I bristled.

"Don't worry," he said. "The door gets most everyone."

I was hardly "most everyone," but he was so full of himself that I didn't feel like arguing.

"It takes a bit of time to get to the bottom," he said as we walked. "How about I use that time to tell you about myself?"

I rolled my eyes, even though he wasn't looking back

to see it. "By all means," I said, since it would be better than walking in awkward silence. "Go ahead."

"I was born in 1897, in India. But my life didn't truly begin until the summer of 1918, when a beautiful witch named Kavya moved to my village," he said, and while I couldn't see his face, it sounded like he was smiling. "Of course, I didn't know she was a witch at the time. She claimed to be a healer from the city, and she'd come to my village because the sickness that had been ravaging the country was headed our way. She wanted to try and save as many of us as possible."

"That was the year of the Spanish Flu," I said, since of course I'd learned about it. "Witches around the world tried to create a potion to cure it."

They hadn't been successful, since no potion had ever been created that could cure a naturally occurring human illness. But it hadn't stopped them from trying.

"You know your history," he said.

"Of course I know my history. I'm a high witch of Utopia."

Was a high witch of Utopia.

Past tense. Utopia didn't exist anymore.

I had a feeling he was thinking the same thing, and I braced myself for him to say it out loud to make some kind of point.

Instead he spun around and stared at me, still taller

than me despite the fact that he was standing two steps below me. The fire from the nearest torch flickered across his eyes, and it was like he was staring into my soul.

"You're more than just a high witch," he said. "You're also a vampire. Which probably makes you the strongest witch in the world."

"It might." My magic tingled with happiness inside me.

Energy buzzed between us, and neither of us moved. My breathing shallowed. His did, too.

Then he spun around, breaking the moment, and continued down the stairs. "Anyway, back to the important stuff," he said, and I hurried to follow him. "Kavya fell in love with me at first sight."

I sighed and rolled my eyes again.

"As I did with her," he continued. "We were inseparable for a week. But the Spanish Flu hit the healthiest people the hardest. So it wasn't long before I got sick."

"Of course it wasn't."

How was he able to sound full of himself, even when talking about how he'd gotten sick with one of the worst flus in human history?

"She did everything she could to help me," he said. "Including teleporting me to the Haven and begging Mary to turn me into a vampire."

"I guess she was successful?"

"She was. Mary doesn't turn humans into vampires often, but she loved Kavya, and she could tell Kavya loved me. So, she gifted me with eternal life."

"But you're immortal." I had a feeling I knew where this story was headed, given that he was no longer living in the Haven. "Kavya wasn't."

"Kavya had no interest in turning into a vampire," he said sadly. "But we married anyway, and we spent every day together until the day she died."

I frowned, since I'd seen it happen before in Utopia. If a vampire in Utopia wanted to turn one of their human lovers into a vampire, they both had to leave the kingdom forever. So, sometimes vampire women chose to stay by their lover's side until he grew old and died.

The heads on Queen Elizabeth's belt were those of her greatest loves.

"You don't approve," Rohan said.

"No," I said, surprised he'd think that. "It sounds like you truly loved her."

"She was the love of my life."

"And now she's gone."

"She passed away thirty years ago."

"I'm so sorry." There had to be better words, but I couldn't find any.

"Thank you," he said, still continuing steadily down

the steps. "I'd prepared for the moment for my entire life. But no type of preparation could make her death less painful."

We walked in silence for a few seconds, and I had no idea what to say. Because I knew women were capable of all-encompassing love. But for a male vampire to devote his heart to a woman he knew was going to age and die?

No one in Utopia would have believed it possible.

"I'd always stayed in the Haven for Kavya," he continued. "But once she passed, I told Mary goodbye, and I left. Roamed around the world for a few decades, spending time with a few rogue vampire clans along the way. Then word spread about Avalon and the Earth Angel's army. Like you, I came to the Vale to enter the Angel Trials."

"And you failed." I instantly felt bad about being so rude to him after he'd opened up about the death of the love of his life. "Or you chose to stay in the Vale."

I didn't see why he'd choose to stay here instead of going to Avalon, but I supposed it was always an option.

"You got it right the first time." He stopped and turned to face me. "I failed the Angel Trials. But King Alexander and Queen Deidre said it was meant to be, and they've been like family to me ever since." He paused and glanced down the stairs. "Now, wait here."

"I thought I was supposed to follow you?"

"I need to unlock the portal," he said. "The process can be... uncomfortable."

"What do you mean?"

"Do you trust me?" he asked.

"I just met you."

"That's not an answer."

I stared at him in challenge.

"You do trust me." He smiled. "Don't you?"

I searched my mind for an answer that wasn't a lie... and one that wouldn't give him the satisfaction of my saying yes. "I trust King Alexander and Queen Deidre," I said. "And they trust you."

"That means you trust me."

"Are you always this infuriating?" I asked.

"Do you always avoid answering questions?"

"So, yes," I said. "You *are* always this infuriating."

"I prefer the word charming, but I suppose 'infuriating' will do for now," he said. "Anyway, you're still avoiding my question."

"Why do you care?" I asked. "After I get to Avalon, we'll probably never see each other again."

Good riddance to that.

"Never say never," he said. "But I know you trust me. Otherwise, you would have said no."

"Why's it such a big deal?"

"It wasn't a big deal until you made it one."

I huffed in annoyance. He obviously wasn't going to back down. "I clearly trusted you enough to let you take me to the entrance of the Angel Trials," I said. "So are you going to take me there or what?"

"I told you—I need you to stay here for a moment." He zipped down the steps in a blur before I could argue, leaving me staring in shock at where he'd been standing.

What in the world had just happened between us?

I didn't have time to think about it, because a bright yellow light started glowing from below. It was like a bomb went off, and I turned away, closed my eyes, and used my arm to shield my face. The light was warm, and it enveloped me completely.

The warmth died down, and I lowered my arm.

"You can come down now!" Rohan called from below.

I hurried down the stairs, into a cave-like room, then froze. Because behind Rohan, a purple vortex swirled on the cave wall.

"A portal," I said in disbelief. "But what was that yellow light?"

"It was a security measure," he said. "We can't just leave the portal down here for anyone to find. As a royal of the Vale, I needed to unlock it for you."

"Great." I stared at the portal and took a deep breath

in anticipation. I'd teleported all over Earth, but I'd never gone to another realm. "So, we just... go in?"

"The portal goes to an anchor island off of Avalon," he said. "To Sir Gawain's Cove. The Angel Trials begin there."

"So you're not coming any further."

"This is where I leave you," he confirmed, and surprisingly enough, he sounded sad about it. "Once you get to the cove, it's up to you to figure out how to start the Trials. Good luck, Harper."

"I'm a witch *and* a vampire. I don't need luck," I said. "But thank you."

"You're going to do great."

He still watched me sadly, like he wanted to say more. And something tugged at my chest, pulling me closer to him.

It was like the Universe didn't want me to leave.

But I resisted. Because I was here for one reason—to go through that portal and enter the Angel Trials. I didn't need some guy I'd just met holding me back... no matter how ridiculously gorgeous that guy might be.

What *was* it about Rohan that was so magnetic? It was like he had a supernatural hold on my heart.

"You're a gifted vampire," I realized. "Aren't you?"

"What makes you say that?"

"Nothing." My cheeks heated, and I shook the

thought away. Because what exactly was I going to say? That he was gifted in the art of seduction?

All it would do was feed his ego. And his ego certainly wasn't in need of any feeding.

He cocked his head to the side. "You're blushing."

"I'm not," I lied, and I stepped closer to the portal, as if the purple glow could cover my red cheeks. "Bye, Rohan. I'll put in a good word for you once I get to Avalon. Maybe they'll reconsider and let you in."

"I don't think it works like that," he said. "Besides, the Vale is my home now. If I had an option, I'd choose to stay here."

"That makes one of us," I said, and then I tore my gaze away from his, spun around, and walked through the portal.

23

HARPER

I WOKE UP SLOWLY, my head heavy and hazy. I felt drugged, and only half awake, still unable to open my eyes.

From the gentle rocking beneath me, I assumed I was in a boat. I breathed in, surprised to find that the air was damp, like I was surrounded by mist.

Where am I? What happened?

Images and feelings flashed through my mind. A beach, a boat, a trident, rolling hills, a wyvern, some kind of monster I'd slain, a dark forest, a castle, and a tough decision to be made.

As I grew more and more awake, the memories disappeared. They were as impossible to hold onto as the mist in the air surrounding me.

Finally, I was able to open my eyes. Just as expected, I

was surrounded by fog.

I sat up—I was in a wooden rowboat—but the fog was so thick that I could barely see a meter in front of me.

Is this it? Am I in Avalon?

I moved to the front of the boat, placed my hands on the sides, and glanced down at the water. It was dark, and it looked cold. I dipped a finger in it, unsurprised to find that it was as icy as it looked. But while I could tell it was cold, the cold didn't bother me.

One of the perks of being a vampire.

After about a minute, the mist parted.

I was in a forest. One with trees similar to the ones in Canada. Snow-covered mountains towered around me, so tall that they looked like they could reach the stars.

My stomach lurched.

It can't be possible.

The mist continued to clear, until it was gone.

I was at the end of a river.

Rohan stood at the riverbank, waiting for me. He watched me sadly as my boat floated up to the rocks and planted itself there.

He didn't move toward me. It was like he was afraid to get closer.

"I shouldn't be here," I finally said, holding tightly to

the edges of the boat. "Something went wrong. I need to go back." I glanced behind me, but the mist was gone. It was just river, forest, and mountains as far as I could see.

"There is no 'back,'" he said. "But there is a grand plan. Which means you're exactly where you're meant to be."

"I'm meant to be on Avalon."

He said nothing.

Because what else was there to say? I looked up at the moon, which was a sliver away from being full, and felt Hecate's magic watching over me. I trusted Hecate, and I trusted Fate.

So why were they doing this to me?

I reached for my key necklace, wanting an answer. But in my heart, I already *knew* the answer.

My destiny wasn't on Avalon. If it were, I would have passed the Trials.

But that didn't make me feel like any less of a failure.

"How far are we from the Vale?" I asked.

"A few kilometers," he said. "Not a far walk—or run. Unless you want to teleport us back. Whatever you prefer."

"We can walk," I said, and I hopped out of the boat. "But I don't feel like talking."

He nodded, then led the way, respecting my wishes and walking back to the Vale with me in silence.

24

HARPER

I WOKE BEFORE SUNSET—AGAIN.

Despite the room fit for royalty that King Alexander had given me in the Vale, with a plush canopy bed far more comfortable than what I'd had in Utopia or the Haven, I was barely managing a few hours of sleep each day. I'd spent more time tossing and turning than actually sleeping.

In the precious hours that I did sleep, I dreamed of the Trials. But when I woke up, the memories always faded.

No one remembered the Trials. Not even those who'd passed them.

Giving up on falling back asleep, I picked up the book on my nightstand and opened it to the marked page near the center. It was a science-fiction book about a group of people who'd been transported by plane to a bleak future. I'd chosen it out of the many in the Vale's library because the main character shared my name. It seemed as good of a reason to choose a book as any, and reading it was keeping my mind off the fact that I'd failed the Angel Trials.

I'd *failed* the Trials.

I still couldn't believe it.

I read until there was a knock on the door. My morning glass of blood, always delivered at the same time by Lucy, a non-royal vampire who worked in the palace. She had a chipper attitude that no one should ever be allowed to have in the early morning.

I placed the book down and walked to the door, preparing myself for Lucy's bright smile and peppy greeting.

But Lucy wasn't there.

Rohan stood in her place. He held two glasses of blood, and he didn't look happy.

"You've been avoiding me," he said.

"I've been busy."

"Busy brooding in your room."

"What can I say? I'm good at brooding." I glanced at the glasses of blood in his hand. "I only need one."

Newly turned vampires oftentimes had less control over their bloodlust, so they were allowed more blood as they adjusted to their new life. But not me. I'd been doing fine with regular portions.

"These aren't both for you." Rohan gave me a devilish grin. "One's for me."

"Tell me you're not inviting yourself into my room for breakfast."

"I can't, because that would be a lie. And if there's one thing I'm not, it's a liar." He strode into my room, placed the glasses on the table, and made himself comfortable on one of the plush chairs. "Lucy's coming over any minute to drop off the pancakes," he continued, as if he hadn't just barged in without an invitation. "I heard you've only been living off blood. And while it's true that vampires don't need food to survive, the food here's amazing. Especially the pancakes."

I didn't have time to reply before Lucy rolled a breakfast cart inside. Not only were there pancakes, but there was bacon, hash browns, and maple syrup that smelled like it had been freshly drained from the tree.

Lucy was abnormally quiet as she arranged the plates on the table. She kept glancing at Rohan, and every time he met her gaze, she looked away and blushed.

"Smells amazing." He inhaled dramatically. "Thanks, Lucy."

"My pleasure." She smiled, as if speaking to him was a precious gift. "Is there anything else I can get for you?

Orange juice, maybe? And some champagne? It's never too early for a mimosa."

"Great idea," he said, and he looked to me. "How do you feel about mimosas?"

It took every effort to stop myself from smiling. Because I *loved* mimosas with brunch. And margaritas with Mexican, and wine with Italian, and basically any drink meant to pair with a fun meal.

But I didn't want to give Rohan the satisfaction of knowing he'd arranged something for me that I liked. Because I *didn't* like him barging in without an invitation—no matter how much I loved a good boozy brunch.

"I have work to do today," I said instead.

He frowned, then looked back at Lucy. "We'll have mimosas—with the best champagne you've got," he told her, as if it wasn't a crime to ruin an expensive champagne by mixing it with orange juice.

"You've got it," she said, and she hurried out with the cart, closing the door behind her.

Rohan leaned back in his chair and watched me mischievously.

"That wasn't fair," I finally said.

"What wasn't fair?"

"You used your gift on her."

"What gift?"

"You know what gift." I pointed to the door. "The one that made her act like… *that.*"

He chuckled, amused. "I have no idea what you're talking about."

I rolled my eyes. Did I have to spell it out for him?

Apparently so.

"You made her all skittish," I said.

"Are you saying that you think I have a gift to intimidate people?"

"Not *intimidate* people." I nearly stomped my foot at how aggravating he could be. He was definitely trying to make me say it out loud.

And I'd worked myself into such a corner that we both knew there was no getting around it.

"Then what, exactly, do you think I did to her?" he asked.

"You…" I moved my hands in exasperation, unable to meet his eyes as I said the next part. "Mesmerized her."

He studied me and smirked, getting more of a kick out of this by the second. "You thought I had this gift after I walked you to the portal to the Angel Trials," he said. "Does that mean I 'mesmerized' you, too?"

I shook my head, like he was being ridiculous. "Of course you didn't."

"Then why else would you think this was my gift?"

"Because you *tried* to mesmerize me. I resisted. Clearly."

He raised an eyebrow. "Did you?"

"Of course I did. You're the one who apparently can't resist *me*, given how you barged in here and insisted on having breakfast with me."

"Brunch," he said.

"What?"

"We're having mimosas. That means it's brunch."

"The sun just set." I motioned to the window, where the final pinks and oranges of sunset were disappearing behind the mountains. Because of the Vale's nocturnal schedule, sunset here was the equivalent of sunrise in the human world. Everyone was just waking up for the night. "It's nowhere near lunch time. And that's what brunch is—a combination meal between breakfast and lunch."

"You're really combative, aren't you?" he asked.

"Only because you're so..." I paused to think of a word.

"So what?"

"So *frustrating*."

Not wanting to talk about it anymore, I walked over to the table and picked up my glass of blood. It was still warm, but soon it would start to cool. We couldn't have that. And, since drinking meant I wouldn't have to talk to Rohan, I finished it as quickly as possible.

Rohan picked his up, but he sipped it much slower than I did.

I'd just placed my glass back down when Lucy knocked on the door and rolled in another cart—this one full of champagne, an assortment of juices, and two glasses.

"Is there something wrong with the food?" she asked.

"No," I said. "Why?"

"Because you haven't sat down. Is there something else you need?"

My stomach rumbled, as if answering the question for me. Because I hadn't eaten actual *food* since being turned into a vampire. And now that it was right in front of me, smelling absolutely delicious, I was famished.

"No, I'm good," I said. "I was just waiting for the mimosas." I quickly sat down, avoiding meeting Rohan's eyes.

Lucy left the champagne cart next to the table. "So you can mix your own," she explained. "I know everyone prefers their mimosas differently. Now, if you don't need anything else..."

"This is perfect." Rohan shot her a movie star grin. "Thanks, Lucy."

She beamed in return. "Any time," she said. "Enjoy!" She hopped around and hurried out of the room, closing the doors behind her.

"You did it again," I said once she was gone.

"Mesmerized her?" he asked.

"Yes."

"Maybe I did." He shrugged. "But I don't have a gift. It's all natural."

From his amused expression, I had a feeling he was telling the truth.

He was *beyond* frustrating.

No good response came to my mind, so I stood up, walked to the cart, and picked up the bottle of champagne. It was an expensive brand I'd only had once, for my sixteenth birthday.

"No way am I ruining this with juice." I easily popped the cork and poured myself a glass, not stopping until it reached the top.

"For someone who was iffy about having mimosas, you're sure going heavy on that champagne," Rohan observed.

"It's champagne—not vodka," I said. "I'll barely feel a thing."

"Is that a challenge?"

"No," I said, since I didn't want to let my guard down

too much around him. "But I bet I can eat more pancakes than you."

"Challenge accepted," he said, and then we both dug in.

As we ate and drank, I ended up telling Rohan *everything* that had happened since Gemma, Mira, and Ethan had arrived in Utopia.

He was good, fun company. And it was refreshing to chat with him. I'd tried to spend time with the high witches of the Vale, but they'd been standoffish from the beginning.

They hadn't said it outright, but I knew it was because I was a vampire. Even though I could use my witch magic, they didn't consider me to be one of them. I was an outsider, and they'd made sure I knew it.

Breakfast with Rohan was the most relaxed I'd felt since getting to the Vale. Which was crazy, since a few weeks ago I *never* would have thought it possible that I'd feel at ease around a supernatural male. But after being rejected from Avalon and rejected by the witches, it felt nice to feel accepted.

Even if that acceptance was from an arrogant male vampire with more charm than should be legal.

"So Lilith has the Dark Grail and the Dark Crown, and Lavinia has the Dark Wand," he said once I'd finished telling him everything. "Who has the Dark Sword?"

It was a good question—one I was surprised I hadn't thought of yet.

Maybe he'd been right, and I'd been spending too much time brooding in my room instead of trying to do something productive.

"I don't know," I said, and just like that, an idea started forming in my mind. "But maybe..."

He leaned forward, intrigued. "Maybe what?"

"We know Lilith and Lavinia are trying to find the Dark Sword," I started. "But what if we got to it first?"

"And then what?" he said. "They'll track it down with that dragon heart and destroy the Vale like they destroyed Utopia?"

His words were a jolt to my heart.

"Sorry," he said. "I didn't mean it like that."

I swallowed down my grief. "I know you didn't," I said, then quickly returned to the subject at hand. "But they haven't tried attacking any other kingdoms now that we have Nephilim patrolling the borders."

"True. But they probably want that Sword more than they wanted the twins," he said. "If they know it's here, they'll figure out a way."

"So what if we don't keep it in the Vale?"

"Do you think you can convince the Ward to take it?"

"Not the Ward," I said. "It would be safest somewhere the demons and dark witches literally *can't* reach. Which means we need to find that Sword, and get it to Avalon."

25

GEMMA

STANDING in the empty ivory hall of the Eternal Library, I pulled off my key necklace and threw it on the marble floor.

I'd been coming here every day for a week.

Each day, Hecate wasn't there.

What use was endless knowledge when the person who was supposed to give it to you was never available?

I was so angry that I wanted to blast fire at the key. I wouldn't *actually* do it—I wasn't stupid—but it was probably a good thing I couldn't access my dragon magic while in Hecate's realm.

I glanced at the door to the hall with the endless shelves of books. Because I'd seen the book that had talked about the Dark Objects. I'd seen it when Hecate had told us about the Dark Wand.

Maybe I could find it again.

No, I thought, remembering the blank expressions of the others who were trying to find books in the shelves, and had gotten stuck in the Library for years. *Don't go there.*

Not wanting to risk giving into temptation, I picked up the key and returned to the throne room in the dragon kingdom where the others were waiting.

Mira frowned when she saw me. "She wasn't there," she said.

"Nope."

Darius's expression went blank. "Where were you?"

"Left something in my room," I said. "Sorry."

Everyone without a key nodded, easily accepting my excuse for leaving and returning. None of them thought to ask what I'd "left in my room."

A second later, they forgot it had happened entirely.

Such was the magic of the key.

"This isn't working." Ethan ran his hands through his tousled brown hair in frustration.

The motion made me remember how silky smooth his hair had felt when I'd kissed him.

Guilt twisted my heart at the thought.

"We need to figure out another way to find the second half of the Crown," Ethan said, focusing on Mira as he spoke.

Ever since we'd gotten to Ember, he'd been back to ignoring me. Whenever I was around him, I felt like I didn't exist. He was always near—he didn't like to leave my and Mira's sides—but he always spoke to Mira instead of me.

It was clearly on purpose, and it took all my effort to resist throttling him and demanding to know why he hated me so much.

"I could try another tracking spell," Torrence said.

"And what would you do differently this time?" Hypatia asked.

"Try harder?"

"It wouldn't change the fact that tracking spells only work for people—not for objects."

Torrence frowned, which was apparently as close as she'd get to admitting that Hypatia was right.

"There *is* another way for you to find the second half of the Crown," Hypatia said. "Landon—step forward."

A male guard with wild, dark curls walked from his post by the window to the center of the room. He kneeled down in front of Hypatia and met her eyes.

Hypatia gave him a knowing look, reached into her cloak, pulled out a gold dagger, and handed it to him.

I watched, not understanding.

Was that a magical dagger that could be used to find

the second half of the Holy Crown? And if it was, why hadn't anyone said something sooner?

Landon looked to Ethan. "King Pendragon," he said. "This is for you—and for the future freedom of our people."

He raised the dagger to his throat and slashed it across his skin.

Blood poured out of the open wound and onto the stone floor.

It was like I was watching what had happened to Harper all over again.

I didn't move.

There was nothing I could do to help him.

The dagger slipped out of Landon's hand, and he collapsed to the floor, into the puddle of his blood.

Then, it hit me.

"His heart," I said, slowly and quietly. "You want us to use his heart to track the second half of the Crown.

Hypatia nodded. "He sacrificed himself so you could do so."

"We'll get to work immediately," I said. "His sacrifice won't be in vain."

"But why was his sacrifice necessary?" Mira asked. "Landon was young and strong. Surely you have the hearts of those who have already passed? Or someone older who could have made the sacrifice.

Someone who didn't have so many years ahead of them."

"The stronger the dragon, the stronger their heart will be for tracking," Ethan explained. "And the heart must be fresh. Once it dries up, its magic is gone."

"But rest assured—we'll have a ceremony in three days to honor Landon and his sacrifice," Hypatia said.

However, I wasn't focused on a ceremony. My thoughts went to Lavinia, who was using Ethan's father's heart to locate the Dark Objects. "How long does it stay fresh?" I asked.

"A heart that's well taken care of can last for months," answered Hypatia.

I nodded and inhaled the intense, spicy scent of Landon's blood.

His heart would certainly be fresh.

I'd cut it out myself, except I had no experience with anything resembling surgery. The last thing I wanted was to mess up and accidentally slice the heart, making it useless.

"I don't think Landon would want us to waste any time," I said, since it seemed like the most diplomatic way to say, *what are we waiting for?*

"He wouldn't," Hypatia agreed. "Guards—take Landon's body, remove the heart, get it cleaned up, then bring it back here. As quickly as possible."

Two guards picked up Landon's body and carried it out of the room. Another two followed them out, then returned with cleaning supplies and got started on cleaning up the mess.

"How long will it take for the heart to be ready?" I asked.

"They'll work efficiently," Hypatia said. "It won't be long."

The guards finished cleaning up, and Hypatia and Darius gave me and Mira tips on how to use our elemental magic. Up until getting to Ember, Ethan had been the only person who'd been able to help us learn to use our dragon magic. And while Ethan was strong, it was helpful to learn from others, too. Especially ones who were so much older, simply because they'd had more time to master their skills.

Torrence and Reed watched from the side, both of them smart enough to know to stay quiet and in the background, to make sure the dragons didn't think they were any sort of threat.

A little over an hour passed before the guards returned. One of them carried a small gold box. He approached Ethan, kneeled, and held it up to him. "King Pendragon," he said.

Revulsion crossed Ethan's eyes as he stared down at the box.

Does he need me to take it for him?

I nearly did just that.

Then, I stopped myself.

Of course he's having a tough time, I thought. *This probably reminds him of what happened to his dad.*

"Thank you," Ethan finally said, and he took the box from the guard.

The guard stood and resumed his post by the wall.

Ethan opened the box and stared at the contents inside, his expression neutral.

"When you're ready, pick up the heart and think of the object you seek," Hypatia said. "If it locates it, you'll get a general sense of where it is. The fresher the heart, the more accurate the location will be."

Ethan took a deep breath, then removed the heart from the box. His hand covered most of it, sparing us the gory details. He closed his eyes and concentrated.

We watched him silently, waiting for him to locate the second half of the Crown.

After the longest minute ever, he opened his eyes and looked to Hypatia. "Nothing's happening," he said, and disappointment filled me to the core.

So much for that plan.

"I thought that might be the case," she said.

Mira's bright blue eyes widened. "If it might not work, then why did you let Landon sacrifice himself?"

Why did she care so much about Landon? She hadn't known him. And he hadn't been murdered. He'd *chosen* to sacrifice himself.

You'd think we'd seen enough death by now for her to start growing numb to it.

Like I have.

"A dragon heart can only track an object if that object is in the same realm as the heart," Hypatia explained. "If Ethan feels nothing, then the second half of the Holy Crown likely isn't in Ember."

"We've only been to two other realms," Ethan said. "Earth and the Otherworld."

"We've been to Mystica," Torrence chimed in. "Although after our experience there, I have no intention of ever returning."

"How many realms *are* there?" Mira asked.

"The only known realms are Ember, Earth, the Otherworld, Mystica, and Hell," Hypatia said. "And Avalon, although Avalon is anchored to Earth. But, might I suggest you start with the most likely one of the bunch?"

"You mean Earth?" I asked.

"Precisely."

"But if the second half of the Crown is on Earth, wouldn't Lavinia have found it already?"

"To find an object, you have to focus on what is it you're looking for," Hypatia said. "Lavinia doesn't know the Crown has been split into two. She doesn't know to look for *half* of it. She cannot find what doesn't exist. And the Crown in its entirety doesn't exist."

"But she can locate the other three Holy Objects," I said. "So why didn't she use the heart to track down Annika, Raven, and Selena?"

"Who says she hasn't?" Torrence chimed in.

Hypatia looked at her calmly. "Go on."

"Lilith has been extremely strategic in this war for the sixteen years she's been on Earth," Torrence continued. "We know she's on a mission to find all four Dark Objects, and that she hasn't acquired all of them yet. We also know she's been hunting gifted humans, turning them into gifted vampires, and draining them for their blood. We still haven't figured out *why* she's doing this, but it has to all be for some greater plan. She's probably waiting to attack until she has all her pieces in place."

"A logical conclusion," Hypatia said, and Torrence looked pleased with herself for getting the dragon Elder to agree with her.

"So it sounds like we should get going," I said. "Get our pieces in place before Lilith gets hers." I turned to Torrence and Reed. "Before we came to the Otherworld, the Empress's advisor gave us these." I removed the portal tokens from my pocket. "The only two tokens that can bring you out of Ember."

Suspicion dawned in Torrence's eyes. "How'd she know you'd need them?"

"Prince Devyn gave them to her."

Torrence nodded in understanding. She knew all about Selena's dad, and his gift of omniscient sight, so mentioning him was the only explanation necessary.

"Any chance she told you where they'd bring us?" she asked.

"They'll bring you to the Otherworld," I said.

"Figured," she said. "Good thing we're on good terms with the fae. We shouldn't have an issue getting back to Earth from there."

"What's your plan for when you're back?"

"We're going home—to Avalon," she said. "The Earth Angel needs to know what happened to her daughter."

I couldn't imagine how difficult that conversation was going to be. "Then I guess this is goodbye," I said, surprised by the twinge of sadness I felt at the thought. Even though Torrence had been dark when she'd saved us from the mages, there was a certain bond you developed with someone when they saved your life. And ever since the Crown had brought her back from the darkness, she was actually pretty cool.

"Goodbye for now," Torrence said. "You never know where the future might lead." She took the tokens and handed one to Reed. "Now, where's the nearest fountain?" she asked. "Because I'm ready to get out of here."

26

GEMMA

After Torrence and Reed left, the Elders brought us the half of the Crown. Ethan took it for safe keeping. He didn't explain why, but I guessed he didn't want to have to choose between giving it to me or Mira.

It was definitely the right call.

We said goodbye to the Elders, then used our keys to enter the Library.

As had been the case recently, Hecate wasn't there.

I walked back to the door and brought out my key.

Mira and Ethan didn't move.

"Are you guys coming?" I asked.

"There's something we need to talk about first," Ethan said.

I stilled, not liking his serious tone. "And what's that?"

"Ever since touching that piece of the Crown, you've been different."

"I don't know what you're talking about."

It was a lie. I knew exactly the moment he was referring to—it was when I'd handed the Crown to Torrence.

It was the ice that had flooded my veins when she'd touched it and returned from the darkness.

But I didn't mind. In fact, I liked it.

It numbed the pain I'd felt every time I looked at Ethan and remembered what it felt like to kiss him.

Whatever had happened when I'd touched the Crown had made me stronger. Less emotional. Less vulnerable.

"When Torrence touched the Crown, it brought her out of the darkness," he said. "But when you touched the Crown, it put darkness into you."

"When I touched the Crown, it gave me purpose," I said. "It gave me something to fight for."

"It changed you," Mira said. "And don't try to argue with me. I'm your twin. I know you."

"Maybe you don't know me as well as you think."

She backed away, like she'd been slapped. "You never would have talked to me like that before."

"Things change," I said. "Besides, you touched the Crown, too. Nothing happened to you."

"We have a theory about that," Ethan said.

"Now you've been 'theorizing' about me behind my back?"

"The change happened when you and Torrence were *both* touching the Crown," he continued. "We think some of your light magic went into her, and some of her dark magic went into you."

"That's impossible."

"So you wouldn't mind if we go in there and ask one of those witches wandering around the shelves if she's willing to try taking the dark magic from you? A more experienced witch, who's able to handle it?"

"It would be a waste of time. We need to get back to Earth and find the second half of the Crown."

"Wrong," Mira said. "We need to get you back to normal."

"I *am* normal."

"Then prove it."

"No," I said, and I walked up to the door, stuck the key into the lock, and left the Library before they could argue with me further.

The Haven's tearoom looked the same as when we'd left. I picked up the pad of paper and wrote to Mary to let her know we were back.

As I was writing, Ethan and Mira came in to join me.

They looked *pissed.*

But it was more than that. They also looked *worried.*

They cared about me. Mira loved me. Ethan… I didn't know what he felt for me. But he cared about keeping me safe.

I straightened and took a deep breath. They weren't going to drop this. I wouldn't have dropped it if the situation were reversed and Mira had absorbed some of Torrence's dark magic.

I'd do everything I could to get that darkness out of my twin.

It was only a small bit of dark magic. Not nearly enough to consume me, like how Torrence had been when we'd met her.

But I was strong enough to handle my emotions without the dark magic numbing them. It was harder, but I could do it.

Because the most important thing was finding the second piece of the Crown. If getting rid of the dark magic meant it would be easier to work as a team with Mira and Ethan, then I guessed that was what I was going to have to do.

"Fine," I admitted. "You're right."

Mira looked stunned. "So you'll try getting rid of it?"

"How would you suggest I do that? Bring Mary in here and ask if any of her witches would mind absorbing some dark magic that accidentally got transferred into me while we were in Ember?"

"We already told you how we think you should do that," she said. "Most of the witches wandering around the Eternal Library are basically catatonic. You could transfer it to one of them."

"I won't do that," I said.

"Why not?"

"Because like you said—they're basically catatonic. And like I told you, I can control the dark magic. I won't force it on someone who can't."

"Then we'll go with your idea," Ethan said. "We'll ask Mary."

"Deal." I finished up the letter I'd been writing to her, folded it up, and sent it as a fire message.

Mary came alone—as we'd requested—and listened to everything that had happened to us on Ember. *Including* how I'd accidentally siphoned some of Torrence's dark magic.

"I don't think you should try giving that magic to another witch," Mary said once we were done.

Ethan sat back, shocked. "Why?"

"Because that magic is stronger than dark witch magic—it's dark *mage* magic," she said. "We don't know what'll happen if Gemma does this. It could kill the witch who tries to accept the transfer."

I should have been disappointed.

But I wasn't.

"So what should we do?" Mira asked.

"I think that question is better suited for Hecate," Mary said.

"If she's ever around to answer it," Ethan muttered.

"Hecate will be around when she needs to be around." Mary smiled knowingly, then looked to me. "In the meantime, most witches aren't either fully light or fully dark. Having dark magic doesn't make someone a bad person. The biggest difference with your case is that the dark magic inside of you was taken from someone else. But you appear to be in control of it."

"I am," I said steadily.

"And I trust you want to remain in control of it? That you don't want to give into the darkness?"

"I don't."

On a base level, I knew it was true. I wanted to help people. I wanted to love. I wanted to be happy.

I couldn't do any of that if my emotions were numbed.

"As I thought," Mary said. "I need you to understand—witches who turn dark do so because they give in to dark feelings. Pain, anger, jealousy, heartbreak, and fear, to name a few. Everyone experiences these emotions at points in their lives. But witches who go dark let these feelings consume them. They welcome the dark magic as an escape from their pain. It's like a drug, and they become addicted. But I can sense a strong soul, and I have full faith that this challenge is something you can handle."

"I don't like this," Ethan said.

"Neither do I," Mira agreed.

"You don't think I can control it?" I asked.

"I know you can control it," Ethan said. "But you shouldn't have to."

"I guess I'm not the only one doing things I shouldn't." I held his gaze, daring him to keep pushing.

Keep fighting me on this, and I'll tell Mira what happened.

He froze, and realization dawned in his eyes.

We still hadn't spoken about whether I'd drank that memory potion or not. But now, we wouldn't have to. Because I *knew* that he knew I hadn't.

Mira looked back and forth between us. "What are you talking about?"

"I'm talking about the fact that we should be using that dragon heart to locate the second half of the Crown," I said. "Instead, we're sitting here, wasting time talking about things we can't control."

Luckily, my twin appeared satisfied with that answer.

"Finding the second half of the Crown is certainly a priority," Mary said. "But first, there's something I need to tell you."

"What happened?"

"Nothing bad, I promise," she said. "In fact, it's good news. About Harper."

27

GEMMA

HARPER WAS ALIVE.

I couldn't believe it.

The weight I'd been carrying of feeling like I'd been partly responsible for her death lifted.

"I can't believe she didn't pass the Angel Trials," I said. "If there was anyone I thought would definitely get into Avalon, it was her."

"Fate works in mysterious ways," Mary said.

"So when can we see her?"

"You will see her again," she said. "But Harper is doing important work at the Vale. Rosella has advised that she isn't to be interrupted."

I sat back and frowned. "I understand," I said, since I trusted Rosella. "But shouldn't we at least let her know we've returned from Ember?"

“I’ll make sure she knows you’re back,” Mary promised. Then, she looked to the golden box that Ethan had placed on the bench beside him. “But I believe the three of you have the second half of the Holy Crown to find.”

“We do,” I agreed, relieved that the conversation seemed to have shifted away from me and the dark magic.

Ethan pulled the box onto his lap, opened it, and reached inside. He didn’t pull the heart out. Instead, he wrapped his hand around it while it was still inside the box.

He closed his eyes, deep in concentration.

None of us said a word.

Within seconds, his eyes snapped open.

“Bring me a map,” he said.

Mary stood and walked to a cabinet on the side of the room. She opened it, pulled out a large roll of parchment, and laid it out on the coffee table.

It was a detailed, hand-drawn map.

Ethan closed the box and placed it back down next to him. Then he got up, kneeled next to the coffee table, and pointed to a spot on the bottom of the map. “That’s where the second half of the Crown is,” he said.

I eyed the spot where he was pointing and shivered. “Are you sure?”

"Yes. I'm sure."

"I've always wanted to go to Antarctica," Mira said with an excited smile.

Dread pooled in my stomach at the thought of the frozen continent. Ice. And water. Lots of it.

"Of course, I always imagined I'd go there on a cruise." Mira tilted her head, then looked to Mary. "How, exactly, *are* we supposed to get there?"

"I must say—I've never been. Nor do I know of any witches who have, so they can't teleport you there," she admitted. "But it seems you already have the answer."

"I do?"

"You've already looked into getting there by ship."

"I have," she said cautiously. "But those are cruises for people on vacation. And they're expensive."

"Do any of the kingdoms seem to lack money?" Mary asked.

"Well... no." Mira looked around at the expensive decorations in the tearoom. "I just didn't think you'd use that money to send us on a vacation."

"It wouldn't be a vacation. It would be a mission. Unless you have a more efficient idea of how to get to the Antarctic Peninsula?" Mary looked to me and Ethan, as if we might have the answer.

"By plane?" I said. "Or helicopter?"

Anything *but* a ship.

"Antarctica is the most preserved natural continent in the world," Mira said. She'd been so interested in Antarctica that she'd gone to a science center near our house a few years ago to check out a special exhibit they had about it. "There are no airports or helicopter landing pads. Well, there are on the research stations, but I don't believe there are any of those near where we're heading."

A quick search on Mary's phone showed that there weren't.

"Getting on board a ship heading to the Peninsula does sound like a solid way to get there," Mary said as she continued to do searches on her phone. "Mid-March is the end of the Antarctica touring season, but I see one or two cruises I can get you on."

"Leaving when?" I asked.

"In two days," she said. "Which gives us more than enough time to work out the details of your trip."

28

GEMMA

On the morning of our departure, we went to the lobby of the hotel in the Haven, where Mary and a dark-haired witch in high-heeled black boots were waiting for us. There was a significant amount of luggage next to them—the witches of the Haven had packed for us to make sure we were ready for our journey. Packing for Antarctica was apparently not an easy task, despite the fact that our elemental magic made us more resilient to extreme temperatures.

"Gemma, Mira, and Ethan," Mary said as we joined them in the center of the lobby. "Meet Bella Devereux, your chaperone for the trip."

"Aren't you Torrence's mom?" Mira asked.

"Torrence's *aunt*," Bella corrected her. "Torrence told me all about the three of you. When the Earth Angel told us about your mission, and that you were seeking a powerful witch to accompany you, my niece insisted I go."

I'd *wanted* Torrence to come, but one of the reasons for having a witch come with us was so she could pose as my and Mira's mom. We needed to do our best to blend in with the humans, and three teenagers traveling alone would draw too much attention. It would also be illegal, even though I was confident that Mary could have forged passports for us if necessary.

"You didn't want to stay with Torrence?" I asked, since they hadn't seen each other for months. She must have been worried sick about her niece.

"I did," she said. "But like I said, Torrence insisted. She said it was a token of appreciation for everything you did for her in Ember. And when she put it that way, I agreed. I don't know how you brought her back from the darkness, but I'll never be able to repay you. She's the closest thing to a daughter that I have."

"Bella's one of the most powerful witches in the world," Mary added. "There's no one else I trust more to accompany you."

"I've heard about this elemental magic of yours," Bella said. "Can't wait to see it for myself."

I immediately called a flame into my hand, and Mira did the same with an icicle.

Bella studied our elements with a determined glint in her eyes. "Neat," she said. "They're gonna love you once you get to Avalon."

"Assuming we get in," I said. Because if Harper got rejected from Avalon, none of us were guaranteed a spot.

"You'll get in," she said confidently, then she looked at her watch. "Anyway, we've gotta head out. If we're going to blend in, we need to try to be on time. Who's first?"

"I am," Ethan said, since we'd already discussed this. The first person to teleport out would only be at our destination alone for less than a minute, and he refused for that person to be either me or Mira.

Bella teleported out with Ethan, then with Mira, and then with me. Our drop-off point was a posh hotel room in Buenos Aires, Argentina. Bella had stayed at the hotel before—she and her sisters used to do some business in South America—so she'd teleported there and checked into the room last night.

Next, Bella teleported in with our luggage. Six large bags for four people. We also each had a personal backpack. Ethan was keeping the gold box with the heart, and another box with the half of the Crown, in his.

"Welcome to the Alvear Palace Hotel," Bella said after

popping in with the final piece of luggage. "Come on. The rest of the group is already gathered in the lobby."

The ship we'd be going on was small—only 140 passengers—and as part of the vacation package, everyone on the trip stayed in this hotel the night before leaving.

We brought our luggage down into the huge, elegant lobby, which had marble floors and walls. There was a huge wine bar, but it was closed, due to the fact that it was four in the morning. The flight to the city where we'd be boarding the ship—Ushuaia—was ridiculously early.

Our luggage was loaded onto the bus, which took us to the airport, where a plane chartering waited for us. The others on the trip were mainly older couples—probably retired—but in good shape. There were also a few families with kids who looked around our age, or in their lower twenties. They were all eyeing each other, as if deciding if they'd become vacation friends or not.

I looked away whenever one of them looked my way. We weren't on this trip to make friends. The fewer people we chatted with, the better.

It would make Bella's job easier after our mission was complete.

The flight was about three and a half hours long. Mary probably could have found at least *one* witch who'd been to Ushuaia before, but since everyone on the trip was flying there together, going with them on the plane was part of our plan of blending in.

More busses met us in Ushuaia, and the cruise company provided us with a tour around the area until the ship was ready to board. We took photos with the mountain landscape behind us, had a delicious Patagonian lunch, and played with Siberian huskies at a local dog sanctuary.

Finally, the bus brought us to the port, where our ship—The Golden Explorer—was waiting.

While we waited in line to check in, waiters wearing white gloves presented us with champagne on silver platters—and juice for those of us underage. The ship went with the American law of having to be twenty-one to drink, but Bella also opted for juice, since we needed to keep our guard up at all times.

Just because this *felt* like a vacation, it didn't mean it *was* a vacation.

A mother and daughter stood behind us, and the mother smiled at us as she took a glass of champagne. "This is my daughter, Vera," she said before taking a long sip of her drink. "It looks like she might be the same age as the three of you…?"

"We're seventeen," Mira said quickly.

"Vera's twenty," the woman said, and Vera gave us a small smile. "Are you triplets?"

"We're twins," Mira said. "Ethan's my boyfriend."

My heart clenched, but I maintained what I hoped was a friendly smile.

"Are you gonna do the polar plunge?" Vera asked.

"You bet I am," Mira said, at the same time as Ethan and I said no.

"Cool." Vera focused on Mira. "Want to jump together?"

"Yes." Mira smiled, and the two of them chatted until it was our turn to check in. Bella kept glaring at her to stop, but Mira ignored her.

Finally, Bella stepped up to the check-in desk. "Bella Devereux," she said, and then she told the woman our names.

"We have you in the owner's suite." She gave us a friendly smile and handed us each a plastic key card. "Suite 734. Welcome aboard the Golden Explorer. Your butler is waiting in your suite to tell you about what the ship has to offer, and to get you acquainted with the amenities on board."

Butler? I thought as we took the elevator to the seventh deck. I knew this was a luxury cruise line... but each room had a personal *butler?*

Sure enough, a butler was waiting in the hall next to

our door when we arrived. He introduced himself as Kent, and he gave us a tour of our suite, letting us know to call him whenever we needed anything.

Everything about the suite was pure luxury, down to the marble bathrooms, silk sheets, and large balcony overlooking the water. There was even a bucket with two bottles of fancy champagne waiting on the table.

"What are those for?" I motioned to the chains that bolted the table and chairs to the floor.

"They keep the furniture in place while crossing the Drake Passage," he said. "The forecast is looking rough for our crossing, so you'll be glad they're there. If you brought the patch with you, now's a good time to put it on."

Alarm bubbled up inside me. "What patch?"

"The seasickness patch," he explained. "Goes on your neck behind your ear. Most passengers wear them while crossing the Drake. If you didn't bring any, you can stop by the medical center and pick some up from the doctor."

"Did we bring the patch?" I asked Bella.

"Too many possible side effects," she said. "We're going to tough out the Drake naturally."

Kent raised an eyebrow, apparently wary of this decision. "As you wish," he said. "The medical center's hours are listed in the directory, in case you change your mind."

From his tone, it sounded like he was positive we were going to change our minds.

"There's a briefing each evening at 6:00," Kent continued. "Have you been on a Goldensea expedition cruise before?"

"Nope." I hadn't been on *any* cruise before. Why travel by sea when there were plenty of perfectly good hotels on solid ground?

"Since it's an expedition cruise, we have no set destinations," he explained. "The expedition crew analyzes the conditions each evening and figures out where we can safely anchor down for our daily shore excursions. Ideally, we'll have two landings per day—one in the morning and one in the afternoon. However, this is dependent on the ocean's conditions, since it needs to be safe to land." He looked at each of us, like he was making sure we were following, then continued, "If you need anything or have any questions, press the butler button on the phone, and I'll be of your assistance. Would you like to go to the restaurant for lunch while I unpack for you?"

"We'll unpack ourselves," Bella said. "And we'll be taking all of our meals in the room."

Kent looked taken aback, but he quickly masked his

reaction. "As you wish," he said. "If you decide to check out the restaurant, it's in the aft of deck four."

"Thank you," Bella said, and it was clear from her tone that we were *not* going to check out the restaurant.

The fewer people we interacted with, the better. Which meant it would likely be the four of us, inside the cabin, ordering room service until the dragon heart told Ethan that we were close enough to jump ship.

Kent left the room, and I turned to Mira. "What's the Drake Passage?" I asked.

"It's the passage between the southern tip of South American and the Antarctic Peninsula. It's one of the roughest seas in the world," she said casually. "The Atlantic, Pacific, and Southern Oceans all meet in the Drake Passage. Throw a storm into the mix, and we'll get to experience the famous Drake Shake."

"Drake Shake?" I wrapped my arms around my stomach, baffled by how she sounded *excited* for this experience.

She glanced at the table and chairs. "It's why those are bolted to the floor," she said. "The ship will be *rocking!"*

"I figured," I grumbled, then I turned to Bella. "Maybe I should get that seasickness patch. I can't imagine any of its side effects being worse than being motion sick."

"Blurred vision?" She raised an eyebrow, and I sighed, since she was right—if we ended up having to use our magic, blurred vision would be worse than having my stomach all jumbled up.

"Time to unpack," she said. "I'm taking the master bedroom. Gemma and Mira, you get the other. Ethan, you'll be taking the couch. It's one of those that turns into a bed."

"Why don't Ethan and I take the second bedroom," Mira said. "You and Gemma can take the master."

"I'll be taking the couch," Ethan said, and Mira frowned, like she'd been punched. "It's in the center of the suite—the best place I can be to make sure everyone's safe."

"Makes sense," I said, even though I was actually just happy that Ethan wasn't jumping on the chance to share a bed with Mira.

"Then Gemma and I are in the master bedroom," Mira said to Bella. "There's one of you, and two of us. It's only fair."

"Deal," Bella said, and I was surprised—I'd thought she'd fight Mira more on it. "Also, no one touches that champagne. We're here on a mission, which means we have to be on alert at all times. We can't afford to be inebriated."

"My thoughts exactly," Ethan agreed.

Mira frowned again. "You all are no fun."

"I'm loads of fun," Bella said with a wicked smile. "I'm also alive. And I intend to keep the three of you that way, too. So let's unpack, and then, let's practice some magic."

29

GEMMA

THE DRAKE PASSAGE was *worse* than I'd expected. On the first night at sea, the ship rocked so much that it tossed me out of bed. I was so sick that I would have had to stay in the room whether Bella was letting us leave or not.

Not even Mira could go out on the balcony to "enjoy the Drake," as she'd crazily said. The captain had forbidden anyone to step out on deck, and even she was worried she'd fall overboard. And Mira's water magic was strong, but strong enough to save her from the angry, eight-meter tall waves? She *might* have been able to do it, but it wasn't something any of us wanted to risk.

At least my twin hadn't gotten sick. She was the only

one of the four of us who hadn't. At one point, Bella had even moaned about wishing we were able to use the seasickness patch.

She and I both. Although the sea was so rocky that I doubted the patch would have made a difference.

It took two ridiculously long days to cross the Drake. I couldn't eat, I couldn't drink, and of course, I couldn't read. The only thing I could do was lay in bed and watch television.

Bella didn't have a key to the Library, so from her perspective, we were stuck on the ship, since witches couldn't teleport on board a ship. The place they were going had to be fixed in one spot. Try to teleport onto a moving ship, and you'd end up in the middle of the ocean.

There was always the Eternal Library, but Ethan insisted we spend the least amount of time there as possible. It was too tempting to walk into the hall of books and browse for answers ourselves. We couldn't risk getting lost there.

As much as I hated to admit it, he was right.

Plus, we *had* to stay on board the ship, in case the dragon heart picked up on the location of the second half of the Crown. But we still visited the Eternal Library every day—we had too many questions to not at least *try* to get answers from Hecate.

She was never there.

What on Earth did she have to do that was more important than helping us *save the world* from the demons? Didn't she *want* the world to be saved?

Judging by how little she made appearances in the Library, apparently not.

On the sixth morning of the cruise, I was jolted awake at 6:05 am by the captain making an announcement over the ship-wide intercom system. The intercoms were everywhere—even inside the suites—and it was impossible to turn them off or lower the volume.

Add that to the list of things that were making this voyage extremely unpleasant.

"In ten minutes, we'll be crossing into the Antarctic Circle!" He was elated, because cruises usually didn't make it so far south. *Especially* not ones that had such a rough crossing of the Drake.

Little did he know that we'd gained so much time because Mira had been coaxing the ocean currents and the wind to help us sail faster. After all, the more land we covered, the better the chance of the heart picking up on the exact location of the second half of the Crown.

"Our expedition guide Malcom is at the front of deck six with a GPS tracker," the captain continued. "Get bundled up to meet him there and see exactly when we cross the 66 degree south line!"

Of course, we didn't go to deck six. But Mira, Ethan, and I did step out onto the balcony, where we heard people cheering on the deck below when we crossed into the Antarctic Circle.

I gazed out at the icebergs sitting on the water in the distance. We'd passed some huge ones during our journey—the only way we'd been able to enjoy Antarctica so far was by stepping out onto the balcony and viewing the icebergs, snow-covered mountains, and the occasional whale spotting.

Bella had stayed inside the suite so far. It was *freezing* outside, which didn't bother me, Mira, or Ethan, thanks to our elemental magic. Bella, on the other hand, had to put on multiple layers of clothing to brave the cold. She said it wasn't worth the hassle, since she could see the same thing from the window.

After taking in the view, we went back inside. Like he did every morning, Ethan took the golden box out of the closet and brought it to the dining room table. He opened it and reached inside to touch the heart.

"We're getting closer," he said, which was what he'd been saying each day, the farther south we got. "Bring out the map."

Mira grabbed our Antarctica Atlas from the bookshelf, laid it out on the table in front of Ethan, and opened it to the zoomed-in page of the Antarctic Peninsula. The three of us—me, Mira, and Bella—gathered around Ethan, waiting.

Ethan pointed to an island on the page. "Here," he said, and I moved closer to get a better look.

Detaille Island.

"That's where the captain's trying to anchor down today," I said.

They hadn't stopped talking about it on one of the few channels we got on our TV—the Goldensea channel that discussed our journey through Antarctica. There were lots of educational segments on the history of the continent, and on the wildlife we might spot.

During my time in bed while seasick, I'd learned more about Antarctica than I'd ever wanted to know.

Detaille Island was the only place we were trying to land that had remnants of human settlement, thanks to the British scientific station—Base W—that had been occupied and then hastily abandoned in the 1950s.

"Do you think the second half of the Crown is at Base W?" I asked.

"I think it's worth a look."

"Me, too."

Mira bounced in excitement. "So we're finally leaving the ship?"

"That's the only way to Detaille Island," I said. "So, yes. We're leaving the ship. Then, hopefully, coming back on board with the second half of the Holy Crown."

30

GEMMA

THE OCEAN WAS rough when the ship anchored down—so rough that at first glance, it seemed like it was going to be impossible to get to the island. But with help from Mira, the water calmed enough for it to be safe.

We layered up in the appropriate clothing—including our bright red Goldensea jackets that every guest was required to wear while off the ship—and left our suite. We made our way down to the locker room where the ship kept the heavy-duty snow boots we needed to step foot on Antarctica, located the ones with our suite number on them, and put them on.

Next, we got in line to board a zodiac—an inflatable, raft-like boat that fit eight people, plus an expedition guide to drive. The waters were choppy, but thanks to our supernatural strength, we hopped on with no problem. The same couldn't be said for the other four people assigned to the boat with us. One of them—an older man—would have face-planted into the side of the zodiac if the crew hadn't been holding onto him to keep him somewhat balanced.

We all wore backpacks, and I glanced at Ethan's to make sure it was secure. His was the most important, since it held both the dragon heart and half of the Holy Crown.

He squeezed one of the straps, as if letting me know he had it covered. Not that I ever doubted him. I'd always trust Ethan to keep me and Mira safe.

Once all eight of us were loaded onto the zodiac, the driver pulled the motor, and we sped over to Detaille Island. The water was choppy, and Mira—who'd taken the seat in front—smiled and faced forward, enjoying the ride. The air was clean, crisp, and pure—untouched by humankind. This beautiful continent belonged to nature and the animals that lived there.

I held tightly onto the ropes, glad I'd opted for a light breakfast that morning.

Fifteen minutes later, the zodiac pulled up to Detaille Island. There was no dock—we just pulled straight up to the rocky ground, the front of the zodiac lodging on top of it. A steep hill with a narrow, winding footpath led up to a flat area on top, where I could just make out the small shack of Base W. Expedition guides lined the steep, slippery path, ready to help to make sure no one fell.

One by one, we hopped off the zodiac.

The moment my feet hit the ground, I nearly fell to my knees in relief. I wanted to lie down and thank every god out there that I was back on land. But I stayed focused, easily making my way up the path without needing help from the guides.

Once up to the top, I took a deep breath of the crisp air and admired the snow-covered mountains stretching out in the distance, reaching so high that they touched the clouds.

This was the most middle of nowhere I'd ever been in my life. If I didn't know any better, I would have thought I was in a mystical ice realm instead of on Earth.

Mira and Ethan stood next to me, also admiring the view.

"Beautiful, isn't it?" Ethan said.

"It is," I said, amazed by how everything here was so still, quiet, and perfect.

Then, Bella joined us. "We're not here to take in the sights," she said. "Any updates with the heart?"

Ethan removed the pack from his back, set it on the ground, and unzipped it. He reached inside, although he didn't take out the box. He moved his hand around inside the backpack like he was opening the box, then he closed his eyes and was still.

Even though I couldn't see, I knew his hand was around the heart.

He snapped his eyes open and looked out toward the mountains—the opposite direction of Base W. "We're getting closer," he said. "It's that way."

"Are you sure?" I'd been *so* sure that the second half of the Crown would be inside Base W. That there'd be some secret passage inside it that only supernaturals could enter.

"I'm sure."

"All right." Mira rubbed her hands together, her blue eyes glimmering with excitement. "Off to the mountains we go. Finally."

"We're not going *to* the mountains," I said. "They're across the water." I turned to Ethan, alarmed. "Right?"

"I don't know," he said. "All I know is that the heart is telling me to go that way."

"We can always hijack a zodiac," Bella said.

I nearly balked and said that was ridiculous, but then I realized it wasn't a terrible idea. The crew would still be able to get everyone back to the ship. It would just take a bit longer than it would have otherwise.

"Let's hold up on hijacking anything until we check out what's in that general direction," I said.

"Agreed," Ethan said.

"Bummer." Bella frowned. "You're no fun."

Mira rolled her eyes. "Says the person who wouldn't let us leave our suite for the entire first half of the cruise."

"That was different. It would have been a bad idea. *This* is a good idea."

Ethan zipped up his bag and put it around his back. "Zodiac hijacking is an option to consider later," he said. "For now, we walk."

"Hey!" One of the expedition guides—Malcolm, the one with glasses who'd held the GPS when the ship had crossed the Antarctic Circle—hurried in our direction. "You can't go any farther than this."

"Of course." Bella smiled. "Sorry." She gave us a look, and we followed Malcom back to the outer edge of the area we were allowed to be in.

He looked up at the sky, pointed, and started saying something about the birds.

"Very interesting," Bella said, clearly finding it

anything but. "We can go over there, right?" She pointed in a general direction off to the side.

"Sure." Malcolm startled slightly at how she'd cut him off, like he was offended that she didn't want to hear more about the birds. "Just don't go any farther out than this."

"Thanks," Bella said. "Got it."

We walked off, staying in the acceptable area, and Malcolm hurried to another group of tourists to tell them more about the birds. Skuas. I'd learned about them on the TV while I'd been stuck in bed.

They loved hunting baby penguins during hatching season in January. They plucked them right out of their nests. I was glad we weren't there during that time, because that *wasn't* something I'd have wanted to witness.

Bella placed her backpack on the ground, unzipped it, and pulled out four vials of clear potion.

"Invisibility potion," Mira said before I had a chance.

"One for each of us," Bella said as she handed them out. "Cheers." She uncapped her vial and chugged it down.

The three of us did the same.

The potion tasted like air. I wouldn't have been sure I'd actually drank anything if the vial wasn't empty afterward… and if my arms hadn't turned ghostly sheer.

A quick glance showed that my entire body looked like that.

Ethan, Mira, and Bella also looked like ghosts. Our backpacks, too, and assumedly everything in them.

"We can see each other because that was from the same batch," Bella said. "We're invisible to everyone else."

"Cool." I hadn't taken invisibility potion before, but it felt freeing. Like I was an observer instead of actually there.

Something about being an observer in my own body felt weirdly familiar. Like déjà vu.

"Now, we walk," Ethan said, and we continued forward without any guides bothering us again.

As we made our way to the opposite end of the island, the snow on the ground thickened. There were more penguins nearby, although we did as we were supposed to and stayed out of their way.

The island wasn't big, so it wasn't long before we reached the other side.

"Well?" I looked to Ethan, and he set the backpack down again and reached inside for the heart.

He was done in a second. "We're close."

"But not there yet?" I glanced out at the water. It was dark, and it looked *cold.* If we were going into another underwater kingdom...

I shuddered at the thought.

"We still have to go that way." Ethan pointed to the mountains across the water again. "Sorry."

Bella rubbed her hands together. "Zodiac hijacking it is."

"Not so fast." Mira held her hand over her forehead to block the sun. "Look."

I glanced out to where a short, flat-topped iceberg about a few meters long drifted in our direction. A beautiful woman with long, platinum hair stood on top of it. She looked like Elsa from *Frozen*, except her outer gear was made of thick layers of animal skins, like those worn by Alaskan natives.

She scanned the general area where we were standing. "Where are you?" she asked.

I glanced at the others, saying nothing. Invisibility potion made us invisible, but it didn't block sound.

"I know you're out here," she continued.

Invisibility potion also didn't hide footprints.

She caught sight of the trail of them behind us, smiled, and the iceberg floated to the edge of the island.

"I'm not going to hurt you," she said, her voice soft and soothing. A light metallic smell drifted over to us—she was a vampire. "You can show yourselves."

I nodded at the others. Because the dragon heart had

led us here for a reason. And this woman was our only lead about what to do next.

If she attacked, it would be four against one. Besides, she already knew where we were from our trail of footprints.

Good thing Malcolm had been too involved in bird watching to have noticed those earlier.

Bella reached into her pack and pulled out four small tablets. They were the same ghostly color that we were —the same empty color of the invisibility potion.

We each took one and chewed. They were chalky, and within seconds, we were back to our visible selves.

The woman smiled as we shimmered into sight. "Much better," she said. "I'm Katherine. *Queen* Katherine."

I looked around the desolate landscape, then back to her. "Queen of what?"

"The Queen of the Seventh Kingdom."

31

GEMMA

I STARED AT HER, shocked.

The Seventh Kingdom was a myth.

I nearly said so, but stopped myself. Because up until a few months ago, I'd thought everything supernatural was a myth.

Why would the Seventh Kingdom be any different?

Bella, apparently, didn't feel the same way.

"The Seventh Kingdom doesn't exist," she said. "It's an imaginary place the Earth Angel said she was from so she could be accepted as a contender to win Prince Jacen's heart while he was choosing a bride."

"It's true that Annika Pearce—the Earth Angel, and the Queen of Cups—pretended to be a princess from my kingdom," Queen Katherine said. "But the Seventh Kingdom does, in fact, exist. I'm here to lead you there."

Ethan's fingers tightened around the straps of his backpack. "Why?"

"Because we have something you're looking for."

"How do you know what we're looking for?" I asked. "And how did you know we'd be here?"

"Avalon and the Haven aren't the only kingdoms with prophetesses and witches," she said. "We have our own. How else do you think we stayed hidden all this time?"

"I think you stayed hidden because if you're telling the truth that the Seventh Kingdom is real, then it's in Antarctica," I said flatly. "It doesn't get any more remote than this."

"I assure you that I'm telling the truth." She smiled again, like she was amused I doubted her. "Come with me, and you'll see."

I stayed put. "How long have you known we'd come here?" I asked.

"A while."

"Days? Months? *Years?*"

"Something like that. But all that matters is that I'm here for you now, ready to bring you to my kingdom."

"It seems too easy," Bella said what I was sure we were all thinking. "Shouldn't there be trials we need to pass, or something?"

"This isn't Avalon," Queen Katherine said. "I'm not recruiting you to join an army."

"Thank goodness for that," Mira muttered.

"I'm also only inviting the three dragons to the Seventh Kingdom," she said, and then she looked to Bella. "You and I will teleport back to the ship—while it's still anchored down—so I can compel everyone on board to forget you were there."

"I'm staying with the three of them," she said. "We already have vampire allies prepared to do reconnaissance once the ship lands back in Ushuaia."

"And until then, you intend to have them think you've gone missing on Detaille Island?" she asked, and none of us replied, since our plan hadn't actually gotten much further than locating the second half of the Crown. "They'll send out teams looking for you. It'll draw attention—possibly *supernatural* attention. Demonic attention."

"Fine," Bella said, and then she glanced at me, Ethan, and Mira. "But we can't leave them here while you handle the crew and passengers on the ship."

"They'll be perfectly safe here," Queen Katherine said. "The ship you came here on is small. This won't take me long. But obviously our time is limited, since we can only teleport onto the ship while it's anchored down. So I need you to take me there—now."

Bella said nothing. It was like she was waiting for me, Ethan, and Mira to make the decision.

"I have a question," I said, and all eyes went to me. "You say you're a queen of a vampire kingdom. That would make you an original vampire."

She nodded, and I continued, "But there are only six original vampires. Five, now that Queen Laila's dead."

"There were seven original vampires. Six, since Laila's passing." She frowned when she said the dead queen's name, as if they'd been friends.

They likely had been, since the original vampires had performed the long-forgotten spell that had turned them immortal together.

"Then why do the others never speak of you?" I asked.

"Because they don't remember me. I compelled them to forget."

"Impossible," I said. "Vampires with the ability to compel can't be compelled by other vampires."

The only vampires with the ability of compulsion were the original vampires and the vampires they'd personally turned—the vampire princes and princesses. It was why the original vampires were so particular about who they turned.

"I'm gifted with the ability of superior compulsion,"

she said. "I can compel anyone—including other original vampires."

I became suddenly aware of the onyx ring beneath my gloved finger. It was supposed to protect us from mind intrusion, including vampire compulsion.

Would it protect us against Queen Katherine's *superior* compulsion?

Bella shifted uncomfortably on her feet.

"We're running out of time," Queen Katherine said to Bella. "I need you to take me to the ship."

Bella pressed her lips together, not replying. Which was a good thing, since it meant Queen Katherine wasn't using her ability of superior compulsion to force Bella to take her to the ship. She was letting Bella make the choice on her own.

"Do it," I said. "We came here for a reason. We can't lose this chance."

I purposefully didn't mention the second half of the Crown, since Queen Katherine hadn't yet specified what she had that we were looking for. No need to show our cards this early.

"I agree with Gemma," Ethan said, and Mira nodded that she also agreed.

"Very well." Bella stepped toward the edge of the cliff, in front of Queen Katherine's iceberg.

Queen Katherine launched herself up with vampire speed and landed gracefully in front of Bella.

Then Bella took her hands, and they vanished into thin air.

32

GEMMA

"The Seventh Kingdom is real," I said once they were gone. "I can't believe it."

Ethan stared out at the mountainous horizon.

I glanced at Mira, who'd barely said a word since Queen Katherine had arrived. "You okay?" I asked.

"I'm fine," she said, although from her tone, she was clearly *not* fine.

"Are you sure?"

"Yes, I'm sure."

I bristled at her tone, then brushed it off. Mira had been moody since the ship had set sail. Being cooped up in our suite had really been getting to her.

Now, she stared at the iceberg Queen Katherine had arrived on, lost in her thoughts.

"Do you trust it?" I asked, motioning to the iceberg.

"It's ice," she said. "Of course I trust it."

Then, she was silent again. Ethan, too.

"Is there something you guys aren't telling me?" I asked.

"No," Mira said quickly—*too* quickly.

Ethan gripped the straps of his bag tighter, not looking at either of us.

"You still have the Crown," I said to him. "Right?"

"Of course I still have the Crown."

I nodded, since obviously he would have said something if he didn't. And there was no place he could have lost it. Plus, Ethan was too responsible to lose *anything*, let alone half of the Holy Crown.

So why were they both acting so strange?

"Is everything okay between the two of you?" I asked the first possibility that came to mind.

Mira snapped her head around to look at me and shot me a bright, forced smile. "Everything's great."

My breath caught. Because she was lying.

Mira and Ethan were having problems—again. Problems that, knowing my sister, could distract her from what we'd come here to do.

And I was *happy* about it.

My stomach twisted, even though my seasickness had gone away since stepping onto solid ground.

"I don't trust her," Ethan said suddenly.

My mouth nearly dropped open. "You don't trust Mira?"

"No." He looked confused that I'd say such a thing. "I don't trust Queen Katherine."

"Me, either," Mira said, although she still wouldn't look at Ethan. "She can use her gift to make anyone do anything she wants, regardless of any protection spells they have on them. At least, that's what it sounded like."

"That *is* what it sounded like," I agreed. "But if she wanted to use compulsion on us, why tell us she had it at all? Why not just use it and then make us forget she used it?"

"Maybe she *will* do that, after we leave the Seventh Kingdom," Ethan said. "She clearly doesn't want word out that it exists."

"Which means she could compel us to forget everything that's happened since she pulled up on that iceberg," Mira said. "She could compel us to forget everything that's happening *now*."

"We won't forget," I said.

"How do you know that?"

"Because I trust her."

"You can't just blindly *trust* her," Mira said, as if it were a dirty word. "You can't blindly trust *anyone*."

"I'm not blindly trusting *her*," I said. "I'm trusting my feelings."

"Same thing."

I swallowed down irritation. Because this was the same fight we'd had over and over again. Despite everything we'd learned about magic, Mira would never understand the power of intuition, and I'd never understand why she couldn't believe we had magic *inside* ourselves after seeing so much magic in the world around her.

Why was one so hard to believe, and not the other?

"What do you think?" I asked Ethan, since there was no point in continuing this conversation with my twin.

"I'm not sure," he said. "But the heart directed us here, which means the Seventh Kingdom must have the second half of the Crown. We need to go with Queen Katherine, whether we can trust her or not. If she tries anything, we've trained enough that we should be able to handle ourselves. Plus, we have our keys. I'm going to assume there are doors in the Seventh Kingdom. If things get bad and we need to leave, we'll use our keys and go to the Haven's tearoom."

"Assuming she doesn't compel us to forget about the keys and what they can do," Mira muttered.

"She won't," I said. "She can't. The keys are Hecate's magic."

"You have no idea what Queen Katherine can or can't do."

I took a long, slow breath to calm myself, since telling Mira to trust Hecate would be pointless.

Instead, I changed the subject, and we discussed the possibilities of what type of magic the Holy Crown might be able to do. The Holy Grail turned deserving humans into Nephilim, the Holy Sword increased fighting ability, and the Holy Wand amplified magic.

What could a *crown* do?

"Maybe it enhances intelligence," I suggested.

"Or allows mind reading," Ethan said.

I frowned at the thought. A lot of people would love the ability to read minds, but I'd always imagined it would be terrible. Thoughts were supposed to be private. A person's character should be judged on what they chose to say and do—not on their thoughts.

If anyone knew my thoughts about Ethan, they'd think I was a terrible person.

Maybe I *was* a terrible person. But I was doing my best to not let my heart control my brain, no matter how difficult it was. And that had to count for something. Right?

"Maybe mind control?" Ethan said, a moment before Queen Katherine popped back in.

She looked us over and nodded. "I told you you'd be safe."

"How'd it go on the ship?" I asked.

"Perfectly well. No one on board knows you were ever there."

"And what about Bella?"

"She's returned to Avalon. She's looking forward to being in warm weather again, so she can wear more flattering clothing."

I smiled, because that sounded like something Bella would say.

"Now, let's hop on board." Queen Katherine motioned to the iceberg she'd arrived on. "And I'll take you to the Seventh Kingdom."

33

GEMMA

THE ICEBERG WASN'T SLIPPERY—PROBABLY thanks to some type of spell. But the moment I stepped onto it, the gentle rocking made my stomach cramp up. I wrapped my arms around myself, swallowing down nausea as the iceberg floated away.

We'd only traveled for about five minutes before the outline of a boundary dome shimmered in the open ocean ahead.

"This iceberg has been enchanted by our witch," Queen Katherine said. "Anyone on board can pass through the boundary."

Sure enough, the iceberg slipped through the boundary with us on it. As we went through, a tingle passed over my skin.

A small, deserted island had been hidden inside the

dome, with a snow-covered log cabin in the center of it. No penguins waddled down to the water, and no seals laid on the ice floating nearby. There wasn't even a breeze. It was so quiet that I could physically feel the stillness.

The iceberg docked into the side of the island. It fit perfectly into the ground, like each were pieces of a puzzle.

I hurried onto solid ground, then looked up at the cabin in question. A soft, orange light glowed out of the windows, the same color as the orbs in Utopia.

I'd expected something grander, like an ice palace.

Maybe, like the huts in the Ward, the cabin was a cover for an underground kingdom.

Without a word, Queen Katherine led us up the snowy path to the cabin. Once we were close enough, I noticed a thin layer of frost covering every bit of the wood.

Queen Katherine reached for the frosty handle of the door, turned it, and walked inside.

I toyed with the chain of my necklace as I stepped through. Because where there was a door, there was a way out.

Three women in heavy animal skins who looked around Queen Katherine's age—in their mid-twenties—sat around a small dining table. By their scents, I could tell that one was a witch, one a vampire, and the other a dragon.

Their scents were complemented by an earthy, meaty concoction brewing in the cauldron over the fireplace.

The fire called to me, the flames leaning slightly in my direction.

"Meet Genevieve, Constance, and Isemay." Queen Katherine pointed to each woman as she said her name. "My loyal subjects in the Seventh Kingdom."

"There are only four of you?" Mira looked baffled.

I was also surprised, although unlike my sister, I did my best to hide it.

Ethan focused on Isemay, the dark-skinned dragon with soft almond eyes. "How did you get here?" he asked. "There haven't been any dragons on Earth in centuries."

"I arrived with the dragons when we first left Ember to explore Earth," she said in a strange accent I couldn't quite place.

"Impossible," Ethan said.

"Why do you say that?"

"Because the dragons came to Earth centuries ago. You don't look a day over twenty-five."

"Incorrect," she said. "I'm twenty-seven."

"It's close enough," he said. "Given that you should be long dead."

She frowned, then looked to Queen Katherine, as if it wasn't up to her to say more.

"Please, join us around the table," Queen Katherine said to the three of us. "We've prepared a hot stew to enjoy while we fill you in on the purpose of the Seventh Kingdom, and our duty as its inhabitants."

I glanced at the cauldron, and while I still instinctively trusted Queen Katherine, I also worried about consuming something when I didn't know what was inside of it.

"It smells amazing," Mira said, apparently not sharing my concern. "I'm starving."

"Wait," Ethan said, and Mira stopped when she was halfway to the table. He looked back to Queen Katherine, and continued, "You told us that you had what we were seeking. We trusted you by following you to your kingdom. Now, I think it's only fair that before we sit down to a meal, you show us that you have what we came here for."

"Understandable," she said, and then she looked to Genevieve. "Go fetch it."

Genevieve stood up—she was tall and willowy, with the classic looks of a Hollywood movie star—and walked into the next room. She returned holding a wooden box with sheer frost covering all sides of it. It was the same size as the gold box in Ethan's backpack that held our half of the Holy Crown.

"Open it," Queen Katherine said.

Genevieve did as commanded.

Inside the box was the second half of the Holy Crown. The small clear crystals and half of a crescent moon on the end were mirror images of the Crown in Ethan's bag.

I wanted to run for the box and take it. But I also didn't want to start a fight with an original vampire, a powerful witch, another vampire, and a dragon. So I stayed where I was, although my eyes remained glued on the second half of the Crown.

"How long have you had it here?" Ethan asked.

"We've guarded this half of the Crown for centuries," Queen Katherine said. "Right after the dragons came to Earth, Isemay came to me with it. She said a fae with omniscient sight came to Ember with both halves of the Crown. He instructed the King of Ember to guard the first half. Then he gave the second half to Isemay, told her to find me, and gave her instructions on what to tell me to do with it."

"The fae with omniscient sight was Prince Devyn," I said.

"He was," Isemay confirmed.

Queen Katherine gave Genevieve a pointed look, and the witch closed the box and placed it on a side table against the wall. "Now do you trust me to sit down to a meal?" she asked. "You know the rules of the kingdoms. Trust must be shown before deals are made."

I nodded, since I'd learned that in Utopia.

Trust was shown by accepting food from your hosts. And I *did* trust Queen Katherine. So I walked over to the table and sat in the chair next to the other vampire, Constance. She was small with strawberry blonde hair, and appeared the least threatening of the three.

Ethan sat in the seat next to me, and Mira took the seat next to him.

"Isemay—get our guests some water," the queen said. "I'll serve the stew."

Within a minute, we were all gathered around the table with glasses of water and steaming bowls of stew.

I picked up my spoon and studied the stew suspiciously. The meat inside was unidentifiable. "What's in it?" I asked.

Please don't say penguin.

"Whale," Queen Katherine said, and my stomach dropped.

They expected me to eat *whale?*

However, I supposed I ate many other fish. And,

more importantly, we needed the second half of the Crown. If that meant trying whale stew, then so be it.

I dipped my spoon into the bowl and took a bite. The meat didn't taste all that different from beef.

Queen Katherine nodded after all three of us took a bite. "The four of us have been in this cabin for centuries, guarding the second half of the Crown so we can give it to you," she said.

I looked around the small cabin in horror. "You didn't leave this place for *centuries?*"

"Genevieve and Isemay worked together to safely freeze us until you arrived," she said.

"You mean like in science fiction when people get frozen to travel through space?"

All four of them gave me strange looks.

I guessed if they'd been frozen for centuries, they wouldn't have read or seen any science fiction.

"When people are frozen so they don't age as time passes," I tried again.

"Exactly," the queen said. "Isemay's elemental gift is ice magic, and Genevieve is the ancestor of the most powerful witch who's ever lived—Geneva."

"The witch who gave her life to seal the gap that had been opened between Earth and Hell," I said, since it was one of the big topics in our history lessons. Over seventeen years ago, the demons had come to Earth in the short time the gap had been open. The supernaturals have been in the war to rid the demons from Earth ever since.

Queen Katherine nodded, then continued, "With help from the magic of the second half of the Crown, they created a spell to keep us frozen in time and hidden from the outside world."

"Does that mean you know what magic the Crown has?" Ethan asked.

"No," she said. "But we've been looking forward to your arrival, so we can finally put the halves together and see what happens when the Crown is whole."

I put my spoon down, no longer hungry.

All I cared about was putting that Crown back together.

"Then let's do it," I said.

"One moment," said Isemay, slowly and seriously. "When Prince Devyn gave me the half of the Crown, he gave me an important message about what must happen after the Crown is made whole."

"And…" My heart pounded as I waited for her to continue.

"The dragon king—Ethan Pendragon—must be the one to place the Crown on the head of the Queen of Pentacles. Then, it will gift the Queen with the magic of the fifth element."

"So it's true," I realized, and a wave of excitement—and anxiety—crashed over me. "One of us is definitely the Queen."

"Yes," Queen Katherine said. "It's true."

"What type of magic is the fifth element?"

"We don't know," she said. "We'll find out after the Queen is crowned."

"Okay." I gathered myself, straightened, then looked to my twin. "You can go first."

Mira smiled. I knew it would make her happy to go first.

I also knew that it didn't matter who Ethan crowned first, since only one of us was destined to wear the Crown.

"Wait," Isemay said. "There's one more catch."

"What's that?" I asked.

"Ethan must place the Holy Crown on the head of the twin he truly loves. If he places it on the other twin's head, not only will the Crown be destroyed, but its wearer will die, too."

34

GEMMA

ETHAN PALED AND SAID NOTHING.

"Ethan?" Mira said, her voice small.

"Sorry." He picked his backpack up from the floor, unzipped it, and pulled out the golden box with our half of the Crown. "Let's get this over with."

He refused to look at either me or Mira.

Mira looked like her heart had been beaten with a sledgehammer.

I felt... numb.

It's going to be Mira, I told myself. *He's* chosen *to be with Mira. They might be having relationship issues right now, but she's the one he loves.*

"Genevieve will put the halves together," Queen Katherine said.

Still not looking at either me or Mira, Ethan took our half of the Crown out of the box and handed it to Genevieve.

She took it from him, walked over to the table against the wall, and took the second half of the Crown out of its icy wooden box. The Crown's crystals glowed, like they were trying to come back to life. But the glow was dim—not quite there yet.

Then Genevieve brought the halves together, and white light exploded through the room. It was so bright that I had to close my eyes. Even then, I could still see the echo of the light behind my lids.

The light died down, and I reopened my eyes.

The Crown was one. Its crystals sparkled and glimmered with an otherworldly light, as did the crescent moon in the center.

Genevieve's eyes were bright with wonder as she stared down at it. "The Holy Crown is whole," she said, and then she pulled her gaze away from the Crown to look at Ethan. "It's time for you to crown our fourth and final Queen."

I could barely breathe as he walked over to Genevieve.

He loves Mira. Mira is going to be the Queen of Pentacles. Mira will receive the fifth element.

Disappointment coursed through me. Because I was more in tune with magic than Mira. And whatever the fifth element was, I wanted it. My stomach twisted with a sense of *wrongness* at the idea of Mira having it instead of me.

But what was it Hecate had said?

Trust in Fate.

I wasn't going to receive the fifth element. But maybe Fate had something else in store for me. Something that, right now, I couldn't even fathom.

Ethan took the Crown from Genevieve, then spun around to face me and Mira. His eyes were more pained than I'd ever seen them before.

"Wait," said Constance—the vampire gifted with future sight. She'd been quiet so far, and the intensity of her tone surprised me. "The fate of the world hinges on what's about to happen here. We need to proceed correctly."

"What do you mean?" Mira fidgeted and looked back and forth between Ethan and Constance.

Ethan refused to look at her. He refused to look at me, too.

"The two of you need to stand in front of Ethan with your backs against each other and your eyes closed," she said. "Then Ethan will place the Crown on the head of the twin he loves."

"Why?" Mira looked—and sounded—desperate to get this over with.

"To take as much pressure off him as possible."

"There shouldn't be any pressure." Mira squared her shoulders and looked at Constance like she was a bug she wanted to squash. "Ethan's with me. He loves *me*. Which means I'm the Queen of Pentacles."

"That may be the case," Constance said. "But we must follow protocol."

"Fine." Mira stomped across the room and stopped in front of Ethan. She stood perpendicular to him, so her right shoulder was in front of him. "Let's get this over with."

My feet felt like they were weighted down with bricks as I walked over to Mira and pressed my back against hers.

Out of the corner of my eye, I saw Ethan's hands shaking around the Crown.

He shouldn't have been so nervous. There was nothing between me and him other than my unrequited attraction for him and that kiss in Lilith's lair.

He'd had a chance to stay with me that first day we'd met in the cove. But he'd gone on to meet Mira, and then to date her. He'd *chosen* her.

Of course he was going to crown her. He was only

nervous because of the second part of what Isemay had said.

If he places the Crown on the other twin's head, she'll die.

By crowning Mira, there was also a chance—a *small* chance—that he could kill her.

Possibly killing the person you loved would be an insane amount of pressure for *anyone*.

But Ethan loved Mira. He was going to crown her, she'd receive the fifth element, and she'd be okay. She'd be more than okay—she'd be the Queen of Pentacles.

It should have been me.

I pushed the thought out of my head, since there was no point in getting upset about something I couldn't control.

Fate had other plans for me. It had to.

"Close your eyes," Genevieve said, and I did as asked.

The next time I opened my eyes, Mira would be a Queen.

"Good luck," I whispered to my twin.

She trembled behind me. "You, too."

The wooden floor creaked as Ethan stepped forward, his delicious, spicy scent growing closer. While I couldn't see him, I could *feel* that he was standing in front of where my and Mira's shoulders were touching.

I sucked in a long breath, reached back for my sister's hands, and held them. Her palms were damp with sweat. She clenched my hands tightly, like she was terrified to let go.

Relax, I thought. *This will be over soon.*

Nervous energy buzzed through me.

I heard Ethan raise his arms.

And then, I felt it.

The weight of the Crown upon my head.

35

GEMMA

My body felt like it was being sliced into pieces. Sliced by the sharp crystals of the Crown.

I screamed, but heard nothing.

And I saw *everything*.

Memories flooded my mind—the memories I'd erased with the potion created by Shivani.

The memories of a life where Ethan had chosen *me*.

The final words he'd spoken to me in that life echoed through my mind.

Centuries ago, most dragons had a Twin Flame out there, somewhere. A mirrored soul they were destined to find, and would search for until they did. We wait to be intimate with anyone until receiving our shifting magic. Because only when we've become whole—when our dragon side unites with our human side—are we ready to find and connect with our twin. Before that moment, even if we met our twin, we'd be attracted to them but we wouldn't know for sure if it was a Twin Flame connection. Our first shift changes that.

And then, the final part:

Every Twin shares at least one element with the other.

Fire.

Ethan and I had always been connected by fire.

But the pain shredding my body apart was so intense that I was going to explode from it. It was like I'd turned to light and had been fractured into a million pieces.

Ethan had crowned the wrong twin.

The Holy Crown was killing me.

I was going to die. The Crown would be destroyed.

Without all four Queens, the world as we knew it would fall into the hands of the demons.

So many people were going to die. And all because—for some unknown reason—Ethan thought he loved *me.*

What had he been thinking when he'd placed that Crown on my head? What must his expression have been?

Had he been looking at me with love? The same way the Ethan from my alternate memories had always looked at me?

Suddenly, the pain was gone, and I was leaning against a wall, in a small bedroom similar in design to the living room of the cabin. I stared down at my hands, surprised to find them intact.

I could still feel the weight of the Crown on my head, and I reached up to touch it.

It was whole.

I hadn't destroyed it by wearing it. More importantly, *it* hadn't destroyed *me.*

So, what had happened?

"Ethan must place the Holy Crown on the head of the twin he truly loves," Isemay's voice sounded from the next room. "If he places it on the other twin's head, not only will the Crown be destroyed, but its wearer will die, too."

I blinked, hit with déjà vu. The world felt like it upended, and I pressed my palms against the wall to make sure I didn't fall over.

No, I thought as I steadied myself. *Impossible.*

The door in the room was cracked open from when Genevieve had come inside to fetch the box holding the second half of the Crown.

As quietly as possible, I walked over to it and peeked through the crack.

Genevieve stood at the wall, next to the table with the second half of the Crown on top of it.

The second half of the fully complete Crown that was also sitting *on my head.*

This couldn't be happening.

"Ethan?" Mira said.

I couldn't see her, but I remembered her expression in that moment. Worried and scared.

I remembered because I'd been standing next to her.

"Sorry," Ethan said, and I heard him unzip his backpack. "Let's get this over with."

"Genevieve will put the halves together," Queen Katherine said.

Ethan's footsteps sounded on the floor, and then he came into view and handed Genevieve our half of the Crown.

My heart caught in my throat, and I could barely breathe. Because everything that I was watching now... it had already happened.

This has to be a dream, I thought. *Something happened when Ethan placed that Crown on my head. Maybe it knocked me out? And now I'm remembering the final minutes beforehand.*

That made sense. Total, complete sense.

At least, more sense than the *other* possibility. Especially since, as I'd learned from the nightshade, I was apparently prone to vivid hallucinations.

Could the Holy Crown have driven me crazy?

I reached for my head to touch it again. Because I was wearing the Crown. But at the same time,

Genevieve stood meters away, holding both halves of it. It was here *and* there.

There were *two* Holy Crowns.

Sort of. Maybe the one I was wearing would disappear once the original became whole again.

If that one was the original. Hadn't mine existed first?

Like before, Genevieve brought the halves together. I stepped to the side just before the bright light exploded through the room. If any of them saw me... well, I had no idea *what* would happen if they saw me. But I doubted it would be good.

Especially if *I* saw me.

The light died down, and I resumed my post near the door, watching from the shadows through the crack.

As I knew it would be, the Crown in Genevieve's hands was whole.

The one my head was still there, too.

Now, there truly were two Crowns, existing in nearly the same space. The implications of that were too huge to comprehend. My brain felt dizzy from trying.

"The Holy Crown is whole," Genevieve said, and then she looked to Ethan. "It's time for you to crown our fourth and final Queen."

I stood totally still as I watched the next moments, knowing exactly how they would play out.

Constance told me and Mira to stand with our backs to each other and close our eyes, to take the pressure off of Ethan.

Constance, the vampire *prophetess.*

Would Ethan have crowned me over Mira if we were both watching?

Given that the Crown would have killed her—*if* I wasn't dead and watching this from some ghost-like limbo, which I still hadn't discounted—I hoped he would have.

In my heart, I *knew* he would have. Because since Ethan loved me, crowning Mira would have been the same thing as murdering her.

So why did me and Mira have to stand back-to-back, not looking at Ethan?

If I got the chance, I was definitely going to ask Constance.

But for now, I had to stay hidden. I had to let these final moments play out the way I already knew they would.

A sense of strangeness floated over me as I watched myself enter the scene and stand with my back against Mira's. I looked so calm and serene.

How had I pulled that off? Because I remembered the anxiety that had been coursing through me in that moment. I'd felt anything *but* calm.

I'd been jealous.

Jealous because I'd thought Mira was about to be crowned as the Queen of Pentacles and gifted with power over the fifth element. I'd been trying to stop myself from getting upset by telling myself that there was another destiny out there for me, but it hadn't changed the fact that I'd wanted to be the Queen.

I'd always been told that I was good at hiding my emotions. Mira had been one of the few who could see through me, and in the past few months, I'd nearly mastered hiding my feelings from *her*.

No one watching would have had any idea of the bitter, jealous thoughts running through my head in those seconds before being crowned.

I leaned forward, since this was the moment I'd been wondering about—what Ethan had looked like when he'd decided to crown me instead of Mira.

Then, other Gemma's eyes darted to the door—the one I was watching through.

I flattened myself against the wall.

"Is there someone else here?" I heard myself ask.

"It's only the seven of us," Queen Katherine said. "Why?"

"I just… thought I saw something."

My heart leaped.

Because I hadn't looked over here before. I hadn't *said* that before.

Just by standing here and watching through the crack, I'd changed what had happened mere minutes ago.

Although given that I'd gotten all my memories back, it felt like it had been so much longer than that. Well, my *sort of* memories. Could they be called memories when they hadn't truly happened?

It was more like I'd gotten my memories of my fake-memories back.

Just when I thought things couldn't get crazier… here I was.

"You're nervous," Constance said to the other me. "Don't worry. It'll be over soon, and all will be well."

Was Constance *helping* me? Not the other me… but the me over here?

Did she know I was here?

Stay still, I told myself, remaining totally flat against the wall. *Don't give the other me another reason to look over here.*

"Okay," I finally heard myself say. Skeptical, but accepting. "Let's get this over with."

I could practically hear the undercurrent in my tone.

It's time to let Ethan crown Mira as Queen.

Oh, other-Gemma. If only you had any idea of what's going to happen next.

Slowly, I moved to peek through the crack again.

The other me had her eyes closed. Mira's back was facing me, but I knew she had hers closed, too.

I saw other-me's lips move as I told Mira good luck. And while I couldn't hear from where I was standing, I knew Mira said, "You, too."

Ethan stepped forward, holding the Holy Crown in both of his hands. He looked at Mira and frowned, his expression pained. Then, he looked to me, and there was no doubting it—his eyes shined with love. Real, true love, just like how I remembered him looking at me in the memories when he and I were together.

My heart stopped, and I held my breath, watching as Ethan placed the Holy Crown on my head.

Other-me flickered a few times, like a failing projection, then flashed out.

"Gemma?" Ethan sounded more fearful than I'd ever heard him before.

Mira spun around, stared at the empty place where I'd been standing, then turned to Ethan. "What did you do?" Anger laced her tone, and she clenched her fists, frost crawling up from her palms to her wrists.

Ethan stared at where I'd been standing, speechless.

Mira zeroed in on Queen Katherine. "You," she said.

"You did this." The frost reached her elbows, and wind rushed around her.

"I did nothing," the queen said, and while I couldn't see her, she sounded firm and resolved.

"Then where's my sister? Where's the Crown?"

"Those are questions for your boyfriend. Not for me."

The wind stopped, the air eerily still as Mira faced Ethan. "What's she talking about?"

But Ethan was no longer looking at Mira. Instead, he was focused on the place where I knew Isemay stood. "You told me to crown the twin I loved," he said. "I did what you asked. And it *killed her.*"

Smoke floated out of his palms and toward the ceiling.

Fire.

The cabin was made of wood. If he released the full force of his anger, it would all go up in flames.

I couldn't let that happen.

So I reached for the handle of the door, pulled it open, and stepped through. "I'm alive," I said, and Ethan paled, like he was seeing a ghost. "And I think I just traveled back in time."

36

GEMMA

Ethan hurried toward me and wrapped me in his arms. Then he leaned back and cupped my face, his fingers brushing against my cheeks as if he was making sure I was real. "You were gone," he said, disbelief haunting his tone. "I thought I'd killed you."

I stared up into his familiar hazel eyes. There was so much I wanted to say to him—so much I wanted to ask.

"You crowned me," I said instead. "You *chose* me."

He nodded, and his adoring expression said it all.

Ethan loved me.

Wind whipped through the room like a hurricane, and Ethan held me close, steadying me. We both looked to Mira, who was standing at the front of the room with murder in her eyes.

Her lips curled in disgust, and she glared at me like she *hated* me.

"Mira," Ethan said her name steadily, still holding onto me so tightly that I could feel his chest vibrate as he spoke. "I'm sorry."

"Why?" Dark anger seeped from my twin's tone, and the frost crawled all the way up to her neck. "Why did you do it?"

He let go of me and faced her, his hands up as if he was preparing to defend himself against her. "I had to," he said. "I didn't want you—either of you—to find out like this. But if I crowned you, it would have killed you."

"You were supposed to *love* me."

"I do love you," he said. "But I love Gemma, too."

"You mean you love Gemma *more*."

He didn't deny it.

"I can't believe that you—*either* of you—would do this to me." Tears fell from her eyes, turning to ice as they rolled down her cheeks. One after another, they broke off, fell to the floor, and shattered. "How long have you been together behind my back?"

"It wasn't like that," I said.

"Really?" she sneered. "Then what *was* it like?"

I pressed my lips together. Because I barely knew where Ethan and I stood. Where would I even start with explaining it to her?

"It's not Gemma's fault," Ethan rushed to my defense. "She didn't know."

"That doesn't make any sense." Mira raised her arms to the sides and shot icicles through the walls, leaving circular holes in the wood they'd ripped through.

Ethan took a slow step forward, still ready in case he needed to defend himself against her. "I'm so sorry," he repeated. "I never meant for you to find out like this. But if you'll calm down, I can explain."

"You just told me you love my sister more than me, and you want me to *calm down?"* The wind whipped more furiously around her, and she rose up to float a few centimeters above the floor.

She'd never been able to use her magic to levitate before. I wasn't even sure she knew she was doing it now.

I'd never seen her so angry. And I had no idea what to say to her to get her to calm down so she wouldn't lose control of her magic.

Nothing could fix this. And given everything that had happened in the past few minutes, I was in as much shock as she was.

Her eyes snapped to me, cold with anger. "You love him, too," she said. "That's why you've been acting so distant for the past few months. I thought you were just consumed with your new magic. But it was because you were lying to me. And you felt guilty."

Her words were like an icicle through my heart.

"I'm sorry," I said, hating myself with every word. No amount of apologies would ever be enough. "I didn't know he felt the same. I had no way *to* know."

"So the two of you were never together behind my back? Not even once?"

Memories of the kiss in Lilith's lair flashed through my mind.

Ethan must have looked as guilty as I felt.

"I hate you," Mira said, and then she shot blast of wind in my direction so strong that I flew backward, slammed my head against the wall, and everything went dark.

37

MIRA

GEMMA HIT THE WALL, and she slumped to the floor. Somehow, the Holy Crown stayed in place, like it was superglued to her head.

Ethan rushed to her side, visibly relaxing when he realized she was still alive.

I relaxed a bit, too. Because while I truly did hate both of them for what they'd done, I didn't want my twin dead.

But my magic was a storm inside me. And seeing the way Ethan looked down at Gemma—with a deep love I'd never seen when he'd looked at me—made me want to shoot icicles through both of their hearts.

Even that wouldn't cause them as much pain as they'd caused me. They were the two people I loved most in the world—the two people I'd always thought I could trust no matter what.

And they'd betrayed me.

Another wave of ice-cold rage crashed over me, and the wind quickened. All of the others had backed up against the walls, like they were terrified that I'd throw them against one, too. Frost covered my skin like a shield, but even that couldn't protect me from the agony in my heart.

The heartbreak was never going to go away.

I'd never be able to look at Gemma or Ethan the same way again. I'd never be able to trust them.

They were as good as dead to me.

Frost penetrated my skin, begging me to shoot it forward so they could feel the sting of betrayal like I did.

I need to leave. Now. Before I do something I regret.

Unable to look at Ethan holding Gemma as she came into consciousness, I spun around, hurried to the front door, and reached for the key hanging from my necklace.

Where should I go?

Ever since getting my magic, it hadn't felt like I belonged anywhere anymore. All of the supernaturals looked at me like I was a circus curiosity. None of them had dragon elemental magic, like me and Gemma. I was different in Ember, too, since I was half-witch and couldn't shift.

I'd never felt like an outcast before. And I hated it.

There was only one place I'd ever felt truly happy. Only one place that might be able to calm me down before I hit Gemma hard enough with my magic to do far worse than knocking her out.

Home.

I opened the door and stepped into the ivory hall of Hecate's Eternal Library. I didn't even bother to check if Hecate was there before spinning around, opening the door again, and walking into my bedroom.

Relief flooded my body as I inhaled the comforting scent of coffee. It was nighttime in Australia, and the shop was closed, but home always smelled like coffee. The delicious aroma of it was permanently soaked into the walls and carpets.

My room was exactly how I'd left it. The shelves on the walls displayed rows and rows of shoes—the types of shoes I hadn't been able to wear since going on the run, since they'd be impractical in a fight. But Bella had told me she had a spell to make any shoe comfortable, so I definitely was going to pack up my favorites and get her to work her magic on them whenever I saw her next.

I walked to the window, opened it, and inhaled the

welcoming, salty smell of the ocean. While it had been nice to be on the water during the journey in Antarctica, it wasn't the same as being here, overlooking the ocean view I'd woken up to every morning for the majority of my life.

I was still looking out when the door to my room creaked open.

I spun around, immediately on guard.

But it was just Shivani—the witch from the Haven who was watching over the café while we were away.

"I thought I heard someone up here." She studied me, and worry creased her brow. "Is everything okay?"

"No," I said bitterly, since there was no point in lying.

"Care to talk about it?"

And just like that, the entire story came pouring out, tears and all. At some point, we went down to the café, and Shivani brewed me a spicy chai tea with the perfect amount of warm milk.

"You've gotten good at this," I said after a few sips, feeling much calmer than I had when I'd arrived. I couldn't put my finger on what it was that Shivani had added to the chai, but it was delicious.

"It's helping you feel better?" she asked.

"No," I muttered. "What they did to me..." I trailed off as another wave of agony crashed over me. The emptiness in my soul couldn't be fixed with a cup of chai tea, no matter how delicious it was. "The two people I loved most in the world betrayed me. I'm never going to be okay again. This pain is something I'm going to have to live with for the rest of my life."

"What if I told you I can take away the pain?"

For the first time since seeing Ethan and Gemma together, a sliver of hope rose in my chest. "You can do that?"

"*I* can't do it," she said. "But I know someone who can."

"Who?"

"She goes by the name the Voodoo Queen. She has a shop in New Orleans. I can teleport us there now, if you'd like."

I'd learned about the Voodoo Queen while studying in Utopia. She was very powerful.

And she practiced dark magic. *Strong* dark magic.

Shivani watched me with an intense hunger in her eyes, waiting for my answer.

"What's in it for you?" I asked.

"Nothing." She blinked, and her expression softened. "Why?"

I finished off my drink, then placed the empty mug down on thc table. Another wave of calmness washed over me, and I felt silly for questioning Shivani.

Shivani was from the Haven, and all Haven witches

were peaceful. She wouldn't have given me this offer if she didn't believe it would help.

And I needed all the help I could get. Because I couldn't go on feeling so betrayed, unloved, and abandoned. The emptiness in my soul would eat away at me from the inside out, until I was a shell of the person I once was.

The thought of the pain to come hurt too much to bear.

But I didn't *have* to bear it. Not if I went with Shivani to the Voodoo Queen.

"I'm in," I said, and relief coursed through me at the thought of feeling better soon. "When do we leave?"

"We can go now."

"Do I need to bring anything?"

"All you need is yourself. The Voodoo Queen can handle the rest."

She stood and held out her hands.

"Shouldn't we send her a fire message?" I asked. "So she knows we're coming?"

"Her shop is open," Shivani said. "She'll be there. And she has a very specific way she likes to do these things."

I nodded, unsure why I was hesitating. Taking the pain away was what I wanted.

It was what I *needed.*

Maybe I'd even be able to move on. I doubted it, since I couldn't imagine there being anyone out there more perfect for me than Ethan. But at least it wouldn't hurt anymore. At least I'd be giving myself a chance to be happy.

So I stood and took Shivani's hands, not giving myself another moment to question my decision.

She teleported us out immediately. My stomach swooped as the ground disappeared under my feet, but the feeling only lasted for a second.

We landed on solid ground, and I opened my eyes.

We were in a dimly lit room with no windows. The walls were concrete blocks, and the floor flat cement. It reminded me of the unfinished part of our basement at home. The only furniture inside was a table and chairs, with a pad of paper and a pen on top of it.

And as I looked around, I realized—there were no doors.

My chest tightened.

We were trapped.

"What is this place?" I asked Shivani.

"It's the Voodoo Queen's private meeting space," she said. "Where she performs her most dangerous spells and delivers her most secret potions."

"She couldn't make it a bit more… welcoming?"

"Criminals of all kind come to her for her services.

She needs to keep the space as safe as possible, to ensure none of them turn against her."

"And where is she?"

"Upstairs. I have to send her a fire message from this room—with the pen and paper provided—to tell her that we're here, and why. She'll come to us when she's ready."

I sighed with relief that Shivani wouldn't be leaving me in this awful place alone.

As long as she was with me, I was safe.

Shivani sat down and penned the letter. Once done, she folded it, picked it up, and it disappeared in a flame in her palm.

"How long will we wait?" I bounced my leg, anxious to get rid of my heartbreak. I kept seeing the moment when Gemma appeared by Ethan's side, and the way he'd looked at her with so much love…

My heart couldn't bear it.

"The spell is dangerous, but it doesn't take much preparation," she said. "Minutes, if even."

Less than a minute later, an ebony-skinned woman teleported into the room. She wore a patterned purple dress with a matching hairpiece wrapped around her head. She was strikingly beautiful… and there was a dangerous glint in her dark eyes.

She held a large, pewter goblet in one hand, and a

matching dagger in the other. "Mira Brown," she said, sizing me up. "Dragon twin of the Gemini prophecy. Shivani has written to me about your plight. The pain you must be feeling…" she trailed off, as if waiting for me to finish the sentence.

"It's agonizing," I said. "I can't live with it. Shivani said you could help."

"Of course I can help." She smiled and placed the goblet down on the table. "Your purpose here on Earth is important. You can't be distracted by such awful feelings. That wouldn't benefit any of us, now, would it?"

"No," I agreed. "It wouldn't."

"This spell is dark, and dangerous," she said. "It's a blood spell. But helping you helps us all. Which is why I'm happy to do it for you."

"Thank you," I said. "What do you need me to do?"

"Just follow my instructions." She held the tip of the dagger to the top of her forearm and cut a deep gash that stopped at her wrist. She didn't flinch, or show even a single sign of pain. Then she held her arm over the goblet and let her blood flow into the chalice.

It was so *much* blood. I wasn't sure how she wasn't passing out from the loss of it.

Finally, she moved her arm away.

The gash knitted together and healed.

"How did you do that?" I couldn't tear my eyes away from the place where the wound had been.

Because witches didn't have accelerated healing abilities like vampires and shifters. That shouldn't have been possible.

"I took healing potion in preparation for the spell," she explained, and she held the dagger out to me, handle first, with her hand wrapped around the blade. "Take a drop from your palm and add it into the goblet."

I did as she said, although I grimaced when I pricked my palm. The blood dropped into the chalice, and the Voodoo Queen picked it back up.

She gazed down into it, then started reciting a spell in Latin. It was like no spell I'd learned during my time in Utopia. It had to have been created by her, or by one of her ancestors.

Wind whipped around her, and a silver glow surrounded the goblet.

The magic felt sinister. Evil.

Dark.

Shivani had told me that this spell was dark magic. But still, it sent a shiver down my spine, like it was warning me away.

Maybe this isn't such a good idea, a tiny voice said in the back of my mind.

I pushed it down.

Because the pain in my soul was too intense. If getting rid of it meant participating in a bit of dark magic, then so be it. And, like the Voodoo Queen had said, getting rid of this pain would allow me to fully focus on doing my part in saving the world from the demons.

I was doing this to help us all.

The silver glow expanded, until it surrounded me. It was icy cold, even to me. It prickled over my skin, and my lungs burned as I breathed it in. Even my bones felt cold.

Unlike my ice magic, which felt comforting and safe, the cold coming from the silver magic *hurt.*

But it didn't hurt as badly as the pain in my heart. Nothing in the world could ever be as agonizing as that.

The silver magic disappeared back into the chalice, and I could breathe again.

The Voodoo Queen stared hungrily down into it.

Then she lifted it to her lips and drank from it. "Perfect," she said, and she handed it to me. "Only take a sip. Anything else will be lethal."

The chalice was heavier than I'd anticipated, and darkness slithered into my palms and through my veins when I held it. I gazed down into the blood inside, inhaling its foul scent. Disgust rolled through my stomach, and I swallowed, unsure I'd be able to get it down.

"What your sister and boyfriend did to you is unforgivable," the Voodoo Queen said, her voice soothing and calming. "I know dark magic can be scary, but it isn't inherently evil. This spell will take away your pain. It will heal your heartbreak. Isn't that what you want?"

"It is," I said, and without further thought, I lifted the goblet to my lips and took a sip. Only a small one, like the Voodoo Queen had instructed.

It crawled down my throat and filled me to the core, the darkness caressing me from the inside out. I'd expected it to be cold, like the silver magic. Instead, it was warm. Welcoming. Like a blanket that had wrapped itself around me and was keeping me safe.

The best part?

The pain was gone. I no longer felt hollow, like I was going to break down at any second. Not even when I thought back to Ethan choosing Gemma over me.

I felt… nothing.

No—not nothing.

I felt strong. Powerful. Calm.

I didn't need Ethan's love to feel complete. I didn't need my sister, either. They never truly loved me, anyway. If they had, they wouldn't have turned on me like that.

But it was okay. Because I was in control of my feelings now. More importantly, I was in control of my magic. I felt it inside me, ready and eager to bend at my will.

"It worked." I stared at the Voodoo Queen in awe. "It actually worked."

"Of course it worked." She reached into her pocket and pulled out two bright red tablets.

Antidote pills.

The color of each antidote pill corresponded to the color of the potion that had created it. And I knew that shade of red from my studies in Utopia.

It was the color of transformation potion.

The Voodoo Queen handed one of the tablets to Shivani, and Shivani eyed it hungrily.

"What's going on?" I should have been panicked. But thanks to the dark magic inside me, I simply waited, calmly, for them to tell me why they were carrying the tablets.

"You've been tricked," the Voodoo Queen said kindly. "And it was so painfully easy to do it."

She popped the antidote pill into her mouth, chewed, and swallowed.

Shivani did the same.

The air around them shimmered, and I was no longer looking at the Voodoo Queen and Shivani.

Two women with pale skin and jet-black hair stood in their places, both of them wearing long white dresses that looked like undergarments from another era.

The one that had been Shivani teleported out, then returned with a long, pewter-colored wand that matched the chalice. A blood-red gemstone sat at the top of the wand, with a few smaller ones below it.

The Dark Wand. And now that she was holding it, I recognized her from the battle in Nebraska.

Lavinia.

The Dark Queen of Wands.

"You pretended to be Shivani," I said calmly. "You brought me here to do…" I turned to the other, taller woman.

Her eyes were a deep, dark red.

The eyes of a demon.

"What did you do to me?" I asked.

"I don't believe we've been properly introduced." She smiled wickedly, her lips the same color as the blood in the chalice. "I'm Lilith. The Dark Queen of Cups."

"The greater demon," I said. "The one who's been tracking me and Gemma."

The one the supernaturals had been trying to locate for years.

The one they were determined to kill.

I should have been scared.

But I wasn't.

"Correct," she said. "And the spell I just performed wasn't to bind your pain, although binding your pain is a lovely side effect of it. Because that isn't any old chalice." She glanced at the goblet on the table and rested her hand on its rim. "It's the Dark Grail. And by drinking from it, you're now bound to me."

"That's why I feel so… numb?"

"It's why you feel so *calm*. So in control. So strong." she said, and I nodded, since that was exactly how I felt. "Welcome to the dark side, Mira. You're going to make a lovely Queen."

Thank you for reading *The Dragon Realm!* I hope you loved the book as much as I loved writing it. I've always wanted to write a time travel adventure, and I'm beyond excited to write the next book in the series, *The Dragon Scorned*.

I've set the pre-order date for *The Dragon Scorned* far ahead on Amazon, to give myself time to write the book. But don't worry—I intend on bringing that release date forward as soon as the book is finished.

To pre-order *The Dragon Scorned* on Amazon, CLICK HERE.

If you're enjoying *The Dragon Twins* series, please make sure to leave a review on Amazon. The more positive reviews I have, the more encouraged I am to write the next book faster.

A review for the first book in the series is the most helpful. To leave a review, CLICK HERE.

Are you new to the Dark World universe?

While each series in the Dark World universe can be read and enjoyed individually, I recommend reading all of the series' for the fullest reading experience.

To start, check out the original series in the world—*The Vampire Wish*. Read on to learn more about it! (You may have to turn the page to see the cover and description.)

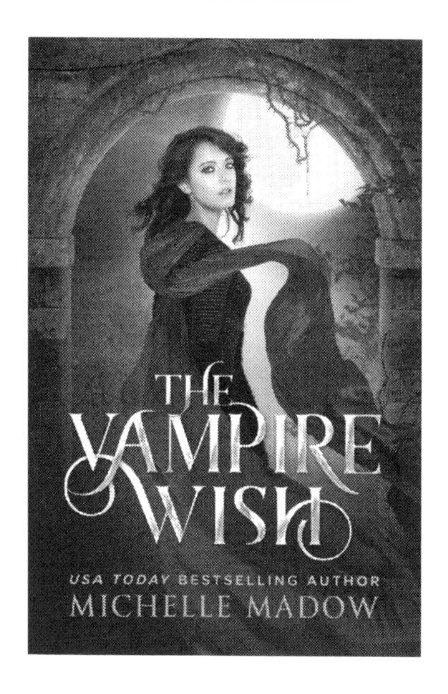

For Annika Pearce, spring break with her family was usually a boring affair. Not this year. Everything changes in an instant when vampires attack Annika's family and abduct her to the hidden kingdom of the Vale.

In the Vale, her normal life is turned upside down. Her role? To give blood whenever vampires demand.

As Annika desperately searches for a way to escape, she meets a mysterious stranger named Jake who just might be her only hope. At first, Jake seems like a dream come true. But as Annika peels back the layers of the mystery surrounding her abduction, she learns that things aren't as they seem. Everyone seems to be hiding a secret. Including Jake.

With time running out, Annika races to unravel the mystery of the Vale—and decide who to trust. With her heart pulling her in one direction, and her instincts in another, she faces an impossible decision.

How far is she willing to go to escape the vampire kingdom?

Get it now at:
mybook.to/vampirewish

HAVE YOU READ MY OTHER NOVELS?

If you love young adult fantasy, then you need to read my *USA Today* recommended series, *Elementals*!

Check out the cover and description for *Elementals* below. Then, keep reading for a sneak peek of the first few chapters! (You may have to turn the page to see the cover.)

Experience the *now completed* bestselling series that fans of *Harry Potter* and *Percy Jackson* are raving about.

"A must read!"
-- *USA Today*

*** A Top 100 Amazon Bestseller in the entire Kindle Store ***

Nicole Cassidy is nervous about her first day at a new school. She's worried about her outfit. And her hair. She's imagined the teacher introducing her to the class, only to hear snickers around the room.

It turns out, things at her new school are going to be a lot harder than that. At Kinsley High, there's something new on the curriculum: magic.

It's not just the other students who have magic. So does Nicole.

She's a witch.

Not only is she a witch, she's descended from Greek gods.

It's almost too much for her to process. Luckily, one of her new classmates is more than happy to take her under his wing to teach her how to use her magic. His name is Blake, and he's sort of her type: mysterious, possibly trouble.

The connection between Nicole and Blake is instant. There's just one problem: Blake has a girlfriend, Danielle. Rumor has it she harbors a penchant for using dark magic. Especially on anyone who gets near Blake.

As Nicole tries to navigate her mysterious new school--and stay out of Danielle's crosshairs--a new threat emerges: the Olympian Comet. The comet hasn't been seen for thousands of years, and it's about to change everything.

With the Olympian Comet burning bright across the night sky, Nicole's sleepy town is turned upside down. Ancient monsters emerge, wreaking havoc on everyone and everything.

An ancient prophecy may hold the key to stopping the monsters and surviving the comet, but time is running out. As Nicole and her new classmates race to unravel the clues left by the prophecy, they soon learn that it's not just their town that's in danger. The Olympian Comet may be far more deadly than they ever imagined.

This five book series has been a perennial bestseller since its publication and has garnered over 2,000 reviews on Amazon, 10,000+ ratings on Goodreads, and millions of pages read in Kindle Unlimited.

Get it now at:
mybook.to/elementals1

Turn the page for a sneak peek of the first few chapters!

ELEMENTALS

THE PROPHECY OF SHADOWS

1

THE SECRETARY FUMBLED through the stacks of papers on her desk, searching for my schedule. "Here it is." She pulled out a piece of paper and handed it to me. "I'm Mrs. Dopkin. Feel free to come to me if you have any questions."

"Thanks." I looked at the schedule, which had my name on the top, and listed my classes and their locations. "This can't be right." I held it closer, as if that would make it change. "It has me in all honors classes."

She frowned and clicked around her computer. "Your schedule is correct," she said. "Your homeroom teacher specifically requested that you be in the honors courses."

"But I wasn't in honors at my old school."

"It doesn't appear to be a mistake," she said. "And the

late bell's about to ring, so if you need a schedule adjustment, come back at the end of the day so we can discuss it. You're in Mr. Faulkner's homeroom, in the library. Turn right out of the office and walk down the hall. You'll see the library on the right. Go inside and head all the way to the back. Your homeroom is in the only door there. Be sure to hurry—you don't want to be late."

She returned to her computer, apparently done talking to me, so I thanked her for her help and left the office.

Kinsley High felt cold compared to my school in Georgia, and not just in the literal sense. Boxy tan lockers lined every wall, and the concrete floor was a strange mix of browns that reminded me of throw-up. The worst part was that there were no windows anywhere, and therefore a serious lack of sunlight.

I preferred the warm green carpets and open halls at my old school. Actually I preferred everything about my small Georgia town, especially the sprawling house and the peach tree farm I left behind. But I tried not to complain too much to my parents.

After all, I remembered the way my dad had bounced around the living room while telling us about his promotion to anchorman on the news station. It was his dream job, and he didn't mind that the only position available was in Massachusetts. My mom had jumped on board with the plan to move, confident that her paintings would sell better in a town closer to a major city. My younger sister Becca had liked the idea of starting fresh, along with how the shopping in Boston apparently exceeded anything in our town in Georgia.

There had to be something about the move for me to like. Unfortunately, I had yet to find it.

I didn't realize I'd arrived at the library until the double doors were in front of me. At least I'd found it without getting lost.

I walked inside the library, pleased to find it was nothing like the rest of the school. The golden carpet and wooden walls were warm and welcoming, and the upstairs even had windows. I yearned to run toward the sunlight, but the late bell had already rung, so I headed to the back of the library. Hopefully being new would give me a free pass on being late.

Just as the secretary had said, there was only one door. But with it's ancient peeling wood, it looked like it led to a storage room, not a classroom. And there was no glass panel, so I couldn't peek inside. I had to assume this was it.

I wrapped my fingers around the doorknob, my hand trembling. *It's your first day,* I reminded myself. *No one's going to blame you for being late on your first day.*

I opened the door, halfway expecting it to be a closet full of old books or brooms. But it wasn't a closet.

It was a classroom.

Everyone stared at me, and I looked to the front of the room, where a tall, lanky man in a tweed suit stood next to a blackboard covered with the morning announcements. His gray hair shined under the light, and his wrinkled skin and warm smile reminded me more of a grandfather than a teacher.

He cleared his throat and rolled a piece of chalk in his palm. "You must be Nicole Cassidy," he said.

"Yeah." I nodded and looked around at the other students. There were about thirty of them, and there seemed to be an invisible line going down the middle of the room, dividing them in half. The students near the door wore jeans and sweatshirts, but the ones closer to the wall looked like they were dressed for a fashion show instead of school.

"It's nice to meet you Nicole." The teacher sounded sincere, like he was meeting a new friend instead of a student. "Welcome to our homeroom. I'm Mr. Faulkner, but please call me Darius." He turned to the chalkboard, lifted his hand, and waved it from one side to the other. "You probably weren't expecting everything to look so normal, but we have to be careful. As I'm sure you know, we can't risk letting anyone else know what goes on in here."

Then the board shimmered—like sunlight glimmering off the ocean—and the morning announcements changed into different letters right in front of my eyes.

2

I BLINKED a few times to make sure I wasn't hallucinating. What I'd just seen couldn't have been real.

At least the board had stopped shimmering, although instead of the morning announcements, it was full of information about the meanings of different colors. I glanced at the other students, and while a few of them smiled, they were mostly unfazed. They just watched me, waiting for me to say something. Darius also stood calmly, waiting for my reaction.

"How did you do that?" I finally asked.

"It's easy," Darius said. "I used magic. Well, a task like that wouldn't have been easy for you, since you're only in your second year of studies, but given enough practice you'll get the hang of it." He motioned to a seat in the second row, next to a girl with chin-length mousy brown hair. "Please sit down, and we'll resume class."

I stared at him, not moving. "You used ... magic," I repeated, the word getting stuck in my throat. I looked around the room again, waiting for someone to laugh. This had to be a joke. After all, an owl hadn't dropped a letter down my fireplace to let me know I'd been accepted into a special school, and I certainly hadn't taken an enchanted train to get to Kinsley High. "Funny. Now tell me what you *really* did."

"You mean you don't know?" Darius's forehead crinkled.

"Is this a special studies homeroom?" I asked. "And I somehow got put into one about ... magic tricks?"

"It wasn't a trick," said an athletic boy in the center of the room. His sandy hair fell below his ears, and he leaned back in his seat, pushing his sleeves up to his elbows. "Why use tricks when we can do the real thing?"

I stared at him blankly and backed towards the door. He couldn't be serious. Because magic—*real* magic—didn't exist. They must be playing a joke on me. Make fun of the new kid who hadn't grown up in a town so close to Salem.

I wouldn't fall for it. So I might as well play along.

"If that was magic, then where are your wands?" I

held up a pretend wand, making a swooshing motion with my wrist.

Darius cleaned his glasses with the bottom of his sweater. "I'd assumed you'd already started your lessons at your previous school." He frowned and placed his glasses back on. "From your reaction, I'm guessing that's not the case. I apologize for startling you. Unfortunately, there's no easy way to say this now, so I might as well be out with it." He took a deep breath, and said, "We're witches. You are, too. And regarding your question, we don't use wands because real witches don't need them. That's an urban legend created by humans who felt safer believing that they couldn't be harmed if there was no wand in sight."

"You can't be serious." I laughed nervously and pulled at the sleeves of my sweater. "Even if witches did exist—which they don't—I'm definitely not one of them."

The only thing "magical" that had ever happened to me was how the ligament I tore in my knee while playing tennis last month had healed right after moving here. The doctor had said it was a medical miracle.

But that didn't make it *magic*.

"I am completely serious," Darius said. "We're all witches, as are you. And this *is* a special studies homeroom—it's for the witches in the school. Although of course the administration doesn't know that." He chuckled. "They just think it's for highly gifted students. Now, please take a seat in the chair next to Kate, and I'll explain more."

I looked around the room, waiting for someone to end this joke. But the brown-haired girl who I assumed was Kate tucked her hair behind her ears and studied her hands. The athletic boy next to her watched me expectantly, and smiled when he caught me looking at him. A girl behind him glanced through her notes, and several other students shuffled in their seats.

My sweater felt suddenly constricting, and I swallowed away the urge to bolt out of there. This was a mistake, and I had to fix it. Now.

"I'm going to go back to the office to make sure they gave me the right schedule," I said, pointing my thumb at the door. "They must have put me in the wrong homeroom. But have fun talking about..." I looked at the board again to remind myself what it said. "Energy colors and their meanings."

They were completely out of their minds.

I hurried out of the classroom, feeling like I could breathe again once I was in the library lobby. No one else was around, and I sat in a chair to collect my thoughts. I would go back to the front office in a minute. For now, I browsed through my cell phone, wanting to see something familiar to remind myself that I wasn't going crazy.

Looking through my friends' recent photos made me miss home even more. My eyes filled with tears at the thought of them living their lives without me. It hadn't been a week, and they'd already stopped texting me as often as usual. I was hundreds of miles away, and they were moving on, forgetting about me.

Not wanting anyone to see me crying, I wiped away the tears and switched my camera to front facing view to check my reflection. My eyes were slightly red, but not enough that anyone would notice. And my makeup was still intact.

I was about to put my phone away when I noticed something strange. The small scar above my left eyebrow—the one I'd gotten in fourth grade when I'd fallen on a playground—had disappeared. I brushed my index finger against the place where the indentation had been, expecting it to be a trick of the light. But the skin was soft and smooth.

As if the scar had never been there at all.

I dropped my hand down to my lap. Scars didn't disappear overnight, just like torn ligaments didn't repair themselves in days. And Darius had sounded so convinced that what he'd been saying was true. All of the students seemed to support what he was saying, too.

What if they actually believed what he was telling me? That magic *did* exist?

The thought was entertaining, but impossible. So I clicked out of the camera, put the phone back in my bag, and stood up. I had to get out of here. Maybe once I did, I would start thinking straight again.

"Nicole!" someone called from behind me. "Hold on a second."

I let out a long breath and turned around. The brown-haired girl Darius had called Kate was jogging in my direction. She was shorter than I'd originally thought, and the splattering of freckles across her nose made her look the same age as my younger sister Becca, who was in eighth grade. But that was where the similarities between Kate and Becca ended. Because Kate was relatively plain looking, except for her eyes, which were a unique shade of bright, forest green.

"I know that sounded crazy in there," she said once she reached me. She picked at the side of her thumbnail, and while I suspected she wanted me to tell her that it didn't sound crazy, I couldn't lie like that.

"Yeah. It did." I shifted my feet, gripping the strap of my bag. "I know this is Massachusetts and witches are a part of the history here, so if you all believe in that stuff, that's fine. But it's not really my sort of thing."

"Keep your voice down." She scanned the area, but

there was no one else in the library, so we were in the clear. "What Darius told you is real. How else would you explain what you saw in there, when he changed what was on the board?"

"A projector?" I shrugged. "Or maybe the board is a TV screen?"

"There's no projector." She held my gaze. "And the board isn't a television screen, even though that would be cool."

"Then I don't know." I glanced at the doors. "But magic wouldn't be on my list of explanations. No offense or anything."

"None taken," she said in complete seriousness. "But you were put in our homeroom for a reason. You're one of us. Think about it ... do strange things ever happen to you or people around you? Things that have no logical explanation?"

I opened my mouth, ready to say no, but closed it. After all, two miraculous healings in a few days definitely counted as strange, although I wouldn't go so far as to call it *magic*.

But wasn't that the definition of a miracle—something that happened without any logical explanation, caused by something bigger than us? Something *magical*?

"It has." Kate smiled, bouncing on her toes. "Hasn't it?"

"I don't know." I shrugged, not wanting to tell her the specifics. It sounded crazy enough in my head—how would it sound when spoken out loud? "But I guess I'll go back with you for now. Only because the secretary said she won't adjust my schedule until the end of the day, anyway."

She smiled and led the way back to the classroom. Everyone stared at me again when we entered, and I didn't meet anyone's eyes as I took the empty chair next to her.

Darius nodded at us and waited for everyone to settle down. Once situated, I finally glanced around at the other students. The boy Darius had called Chris smiled at me, a girl with platinum hair filed her nails under the table, and the girl next to her looked like she was about to fall asleep. They were all typical high school students waiting for class to end.

But my eyes stopped at the end of the row on a guy with dark shaggy hair. His designer jeans and black leather jacket made him look like he'd come straight from a modeling shoot, and the casual way he leaned back in his chair exuded confidence and a carefree attitude. Then his gaze met mine, and goosebumps rose over my skin. His eyes were a startling shade of burnt brown, and they were soft, but calculating. Like he was trying to figure me out.

Kate rested an elbow on the table and leaned closer to me. "Don't even think about it," she whispered, and I yanked my gaze away from his, my cheeks flushing at the realization that I'd been caught staring at him. "That's Blake Carter. He's been dating Danielle Emerson since last year. She's the one to his left."

Not wanting to stare again, I glanced at Danielle from the corner of my eye. Her chestnut hair was supermodel thick, her ocean blue eyes were so bright that I wondered if they were colored contacts, and her black v-neck shirt dropped as low as possible without being overly inappropriate for school.

Of course Blake had a girlfriend, and she was beautiful. I never stood a chance.

"As I said earlier, we're going to review the energy colors and what they mean," Darius said, interrupting my thoughts. "But before we begin, who can explain to Nicole how we use energy?"

I sunk down in my seat, hating that the attention had been brought back to me. Luckily, the athletic boy next to Kate who'd said the thing earlier about magic not being a trick raised his hand.

"Chris," Darius called on him. "Go ahead."

Chris pushed his hair off his forehead and faced me.

His t-shirt featured an angry storm cloud holding a lighting bolt like a baseball bat, with "Trenton Thunder" written below it. It was goofy, and not a sports team that I'd ever heard of. But his boyish grin and rounded cheeks made him attractive in a cute way. Not in the same "stop what you're doing because I'm walking in your direction" way as Blake, but he definitely would have gotten attention from the girls at my old school.

"There's energy everywhere." Chris moved his hands in a giant arc above his head to demonstrate. "Humans know that energy exists—they've harnessed it for electronics. The difference between us and humans is that we have the power to tap into energy and use it ourselves, and humans don't." He smiled at me, as if I was supposed to understand what he meant. "Make sense?"

"Not really," I said. "Sorry."

"It's easier if you relate it to something familiar," he said, speaking faster. "What happens to the handle of a metal spoon when you leave it in boiling water?"

"It gets hot?" I said it as a question. This was stuff people learned in fifth grade science—not high school homeroom.

"And what happens when it's plastic?"

"It doesn't get hot," I said slowly. "It stays room temperature."

"Exactly." He grinned at me like I'd just solved an astrophysics mathematical equation. "Humans are like plastic. Even if they're immersed in energy, they can't conduct it. Witches are like metal. We have the ability to absorb energy and control it as we want."

"So, how do we take in this energy?" I asked, since I might as well humor him.

"Through our hands." Chris turned his palms up, closed his eyes, and took a deep breath. He looked like a meditating Buddha. Students snickered, and Chris re-opened his eyes, pushed his sleeves up, and sat back in his chair.

"O-o-kay." I elongated the word, smiling and laughing along with everyone else.

Darius cleared his throat, and everyone calmed down. "We can conduct energy from the Universe into our bodies," he said, his voice full of authority. Chills passed through me, and even though I still didn't believe any of this, I sat back to listen. "Once we've harnessed it, we can use it as we like. Think of energy like light. It contains different colors, each relating to an aspect of life. I've written them on the board. The most basic exercise we learn in this class is to sense this energy and absorb it. Just open your mind, envision the color you're focusing on, and picture it entering your body through your palms."

I rotated my hand to look at my palm. It looked normal—not like it was about to open up and absorb energy from the Universe.

"We're going to do a meditation session," Darius continued. "Everyone should pick a color from the board and picture it as energy entering your palms. Keep it simple and absorb the energy—don't push it back out into the Universe. This exercise is for practice and self-improvement." He looked at me, a hint of challenge in his eyes. "Now, please pick a color and begin."

I looked around the room to see what others were doing. Most people already had their eyes closed, the muscles in their faces calm and relaxed. They were really getting into this. As if they truly believed it.

If I didn't at least *look* like I was trying, I would stand out—again. So I might as well go along with it and pretend.

I re-examined the board and skimmed through the "meanings" of the colors. Red caught my attention first. It apparently increased confidence, courage, and love, along with attraction and desire. The prospect made me glance at Blake, who sat still with his eyes closed, his lips set in a line of concentration.

But he was out of my league *and* he had a girlfriend. I shouldn't waste my time hoping for anything to happen between us.

Instead, I read through the other colors and settled on green. It supposedly brought growth, success, and luck, along with helping a person open their mind, become more aware of options, and choose a good path. Those were all things I needed right now.

I opened my palms towards the ceiling and closed my eyes. Once comfortable, I steadied my breathing and tried clearing my mind.

Then there was the question of how to "channel" a color. Picturing it seemed like a good start, so I imagined myself pulling green out of the air, the color glowing with life. A soft hum filled my ears as it expanded and pushed against me, like waves crashing over my skin. The palms of my hands tingled, and the energy flowed through my body, joining with my blood as it pumped through my veins. It streamed up my arms, moved down to my stomach, and poured down to my toes. Green glowed behind my eyelids, and I kept gathering it and gathering it until it grew so much that it had nowhere else to go.

Then it pushed its way out of my palms with such force that it must have lit up the entire room.

3

THE BELL RANG, and my eyes snapped open, the classroom coming into focus. I looked around, taking in the scuffed tiled floor, the chalkboard covered with writing, the white plaster walls, and the lack of windows. Everything looked normal. Unchanged. There was no proof that anything I'd just felt had been more than a figment of my imagination.

But that energy flowing through my body had been so *real.* I tightened my hands into fists and opened them back up, but only a soft tingle remained. Then it disappeared completely.

Kate stood up, dropped her backpack on her chair, and studied me. "I'm guessing from the look on your face that it worked," she said.

"I don't know." I shrugged and picked up my bag.

"I'm not sure what was supposed to happen." I met her eyes and managed a small smile, since it wasn't exactly a lie.

But the energy I'd felt around me was unlike anything I'd ever experienced. Which meant my imagination was running out of control. Because there was no proof that I'd done anything. What I'd "experienced" had existed only in my head. Right?

Kate glanced at her watch. "What class do you have first?"

I pulled out my schedule. "Honors Biology." I scrunched my nose at the prospect. "They put me in all honors classes, and I have no idea why. I was in regular classes at my old school."

"I've got Honors Bio, too," she said. "Come on. I'll explain the whole honors thing on the way there."

I followed Kate down the hallway, although I kept bumping into people, since my mind was spinning after what had happened in homeroom. I'd felt something during that meditation session. Maybe it was the energy that Darius was talking about. And if this energy stuff *was* the reason behind the miraculous recovery of my torn tendon and the healed scar …

I pushed the thought away. There had to be another explanation. One that made *sense.*

Kate edged closer to the wall to give me space to

walk next to her. "So, about the honors classes," she said, lowering her voice. "You saw what was written on the board. Each color has a different meaning. Once we learn how to harness energy properly, we can use the different colors to help us ... do things."

"What kind of things?" I asked.

"Let's take yellow—my personal favorite—as an example," she said. "Yellow increases focus and helps us remember information. If you channel yellow energy before studying for a test, it won't take as long to review everything, and you'll remember more. It'll make your memory almost photographic. Pretty cool, right?"

"It does sound useful," I agreed. "Although I'm still not buying all this colors and energy stuff."

"Give it time." Kate smiled, as if she knew something I didn't, and stopped in front of a classroom door. "We're here. Want to sit with me?" She led the way to a table in the front, and I followed, even though front and center wasn't my thing. "I'll help you with the basics after school," she offered. "You got the hang of channeling energy pretty quickly, so it shouldn't be hard. Sometimes it takes the freshmen months to gather enough energy to feel anything significant. It was obvious from where I was sitting that you did it on your first try. That was pretty impressive."

"I'm not sure I actually did anything, but sure, I'll

study with you after school," I said. Even though this energy stuff sounded crazy, it was nice of Kate to reach out. I didn't want to miss the chance to make my first friend here. "I could definitely use help getting caught up with my classes."

"Great." Kate beamed. "I'm sure you'll pick it up quickly."

More students piled in, a few of them people I recognized from homeroom. Then, just as I'd started to think it was stupid to hope he would also be in this class, Blake strolled inside, with Danielle trailing close behind.

His eyes met mine, and my breath caught, taken aback by how he'd noticed me again. But he couldn't be interested in me like *that*. It was probably just because I was new. And because, as embarrassing as it was to admit, he'd caught me staring at him. So I opened my textbook to the chapter that Kate already had open, focusing on a section on dominant and recessive genes as if it were the most fascinating thing I'd ever read in my life.

"I told you in homeroom that he's taken, remember?" Kate whispered once Blake and Danielle were far enough away.

My cheeks heated. "Was it that obvious?"

"That you were checking him out?" Kate asked, and I

nodded, despite how humiliating it was that she'd noticed. "Yeah."

"I'm not doing it on purpose," I said. "I know that he has a girlfriend. I would never try anything, I promise. But … have you seen him? It was hard not to at least *look*."

"I know you're not doing it on purpose," she said. "He's one of the hottest guys in the school—I get that. But Danielle doesn't take it too kindly when girls flirt with Blake. Or check out Blake. Or even look like they're *interested* in Blake. It's in your best interest to keep your distance from both of them. Trust me."

I was about to ask why, but before I could, the bell rang and class began.

4

THE OTHER SOPHOMORES from homeroom were in most of my classes, and Kate sat with me in each one, including lunch. I was so behind in the honors courses that I seriously needed whatever Kate said she would teach me after school to help.

"What class do you have next?" Kate asked as we packed our bags after advanced Spanish.

I pulled my schedule out of my pocket. "Ceramics." I groaned. I wasn't awful at art, but I would have preferred a music elective, since music was always my favorite class. "What about you?"

"Theatre," she answered, tucking her hair behind her ears. "I want to be in the school play this spring, but I always get nervous on stage. Hopefully the class will help."

"You'll get in," I said. "Besides, can't you use that witchy energy stuff to convince the teacher to give you the part you want? Or mess up other people during their auditions so they don't get the leads?"

Her eyes darted around the hall, and she leaned in closer, lowering her voice. "We don't use our powers to take advantage of others," she said. "I'll fill you in on everything later. Okay?"

I nodded and followed her through the art wing, resisting the urge to ask her more right now. Instead, I looked around. Student paintings decorated the walls, and what sounded like a flute solo came from a room close by. Kate stopped in front of the double doors that led to the theatre. "This is me," she said. "The ceramics room is upstairs—you shouldn't miss it."

We split ways, and like Kate had told me, the ceramics room was easy to find. Kilns lined the side wall, pottery wheels were on the other end, bricks of clay were stacked in shelves in the back, and the huge windows were a welcome change from the stuffy classrooms I'd been in so far.

I looked around to see if anyone seemed receptive to having the new girl join them, and my eyes stopped when they reached Blake's. He sat at the table furthest away, leaning back in his seat with his legs outstretched. The chairs next to him were empty. He nodded at me, as if acknowledging me as a member of a special club, and I noticed that no one else from homeroom was in this class. Could he be inviting me to sit with him?

Since everyone from homeroom seemed to stick together, I took that as a yes and walked toward Blake's table, my pulse quickening with every step. I remembered what Kate had told me earlier about Danielle—how she was crazy possessive over Blake—but Danielle wasn't here. And Blake was the only person who wanted me to join him. Refusing would be rude.

He moved his legs to give me room, and I settled in the seat next to him. His deep, liquid eyes had various shades of reddish brown running through them, and he was watching me as if he was waiting for me to say something. I swallowed, not sure how to start, and settled on the obvious.

"Hi." My heart pounded so hard I feared he could hear it. "You're in my homeroom, right?"

"Yep," he said smoothly. "We also have biology, history, and Spanish together." He counted off each on his fingers. "And given that you're in Darius's homeroom, it's safe to say that you have Greek mythology with me next period as well. I'm Blake."

"Nicole," I introduced myself, even though Darius had already done so in front of the class this morning. "I heard that all of the sophomores in our homeroom have to take Greek mythology. Luckily I read *The Odyssey* in English last year, so I shouldn't be totally lost."

"There's a reason we're required to take Greek mythology." He scooted closer to me, as if about to tell me a secret, and I leaned forward in anticipation. "Did you know that we—meaning everyone in our homeroom—are descended from the Greek gods?"

I arched an eyebrow. "Like Zeus and all of them living in a castle on the clouds?" I asked.

"Exactly." He smirked. "Except that they're referred to as the Olympians, and they call their 'castle in the clouds' Mount Olympus."

"So you're saying that we're *gods*?"

"We're not gods." He smiled and shook his head. "But we have 'diluted god blood' in us. It's what gives us our powers."

"Right." I wasn't sure how else to respond, and I looked down at the table. Was he playing a joke on me? Trying to see how gullible the new kid could be?

"What's wrong?" He watched me so intensely—so seriously—that I knew he was truly concerned.

"The truth?" I asked, and he nodded, his gaze locked on mine. So I took a deep breath, and said, "Everything from our homeroom sounds crazy to me. But you're all so serious about it that I'm starting to think you actually believe it."

"It's a lot to take in at once," he said.

"That's the understatement of the day." I flaked a piece of dried clay off the table with my thumbnail. "But Kate offered to teach me some stuff after school, and she's been really nice by taking me around all day, so I told her I would listen to her."

"Kate's a rule follower," Blake said, crossing his arms. "She's only going to tell you about a fraction of the stuff we can do. But stay in homeroom with us, and maybe my friends and I will show you how to have *real* fun with our abilities."

The teacher walked inside before I could respond, and the chattering in the room quieted. As much as I wanted to ask Blake what he meant, I couldn't right now. We weren't supposed to talk about our abilities when humans could hear.

Then I realized: I'd thought of other people as "humans," like I wasn't one of them anymore.

The scary thing was—I might be starting to believe it.

Keep reading Elementals!

ABOUT THE AUTHOR

Michelle Madow is a USA Today bestselling author of fast-paced fantasy novels that will leave you turning the pages wanting more! Her books are full of magic, adventure, romance, and twists you'll never see coming.

Michelle grew up in Maryland, and now lives in Florida. She's loved reading for as long as she can remember. She wrote her first book in her junior year of college and hasn't stopped writing since! She also loves traveling, and has been to all seven continents. Someday, she hopes to travel the world for a year on a cruise ship.

She loves hanging out with her readers in her Facebook group. CLICK HERE to join the group and start chatting with Michelle and her other readers!

Click here or visit author.to/MichelleMadow to view a full list of Michelle's novels on Amazon.

To get free books, exclusive content, and instant updates from Michelle, visit www.michellemadow.com/subscribe and subscribe to her newsletter now!

THE DRAGON REALM

Published by Dreamscape Publishing

ISBN: 9798713542009

❀ Created with Vellum

Printed in Great Britain
by Amazon